# Letting You Go

S.L. STERLING

Letting You Go

Copyright © 2023 by S.L. Sterling



ISBN: 978-1-989566-71-8

Paperback ISBN: 978-1-989566-72-5

Harcover ISBN: 978-1-989566-73-2

Editor: Brandi Aquino, Editing Done Write

Cover Design: Thunderstruck Cover Design

# Bailey

August

I pulled the black dress I had purchased earlier this week from the closet and lay it out on the bed. It was a little sexier than what I'd normally go with, but I figured tonight, of all nights called for a little more. I ran my hand over the silky material, my nerves getting the better of me. It was much sexier than what I'd normally wear, and I was more than a little nervous to wear it.

I'd only decided on it after my friend Justine had talked me into it. I'd sent her a picture of me wearing the dress and the eye-popping emoji followed by a heart had made me laugh. That was when my mind went back to the conversation I'd had with her a few weeks ago.

*"I have a feeling that he is going to pop the big question to you on your anniversary,"* Justine whispered excitedly to me one night at our book club.

*"Really? What makes you say that?"*

*"Well, I saw him in a jewelry store downtown the other day. I was going to go over and say hello, but as I got closer, I noticed he was looking at the engagement rings. I was afraid I may scare him away from doing what you've been waiting for, so I left."* She grabbed my hands, and we both squealed with excitement.

*"And what have I been waiting for?" I asked.*

*Justine looked at me and smiled, "You've been waiting for him to get his act together and ask you to marry him, before she finds someone else."*

*I could feel my cheeks heat at her words and I wouldn't have said I'd been waiting, but a commitment of some sort would be nice.*

I'd acted casually when I'd seen Jim the next day, even though I was busting inside, wanting to know if, in fact, it was going to happen. As the weeks passed, I shrugged off the idea. There was no point in building the idea up in my mind only to get let down because we'd never really talked about marriage. Then one night during dinner, Jim started asking me questions about what types of diamond cuts and ring settings I liked. He even asked me to flip through a few web pages and point them out. As I surfed through the pages, I couldn't keep my thoughts from drifting back to the conversation with Justine. A week later, he started asking me about vacation spots. *"Could be anywhere: Aruba, Antigua, Grand Cayman?"*

This convinced me that Justine had been right. As we drew closer to our anniversary, I figured that would be the night he'd ask, and I'd say yes. As the date drew closer, he'd suggested having dinner at an upscale steakhouse just outside of town. That was when my excitement really built. I was so sure that tonight would be the night that he would indeed pop the question I had run out and spent close to two hundred dollars on this dress. I'd recently lost my job because of the company downsizing and really couldn't afford to purchase it, but I wanted to look amazing for him.

Running my hands over the silky material again, I smiled to myself. Grabbing the towel that lay beside it on the bed, I was just about to the bathroom door when the phone rang.

"Hello." I sat down on the edge of my bed and sat the towel beside me.

"Hey, beautiful! What are you doing?" a familiar voice sang into the phone.

"Cara! What a great surprise! I'm good. How are you?"

"I'm great. I was just getting ready for our date

tonight, and I thought I had better call and wish my girl a happy anniversary." She giggled.

"Well, sweets, thank you, but really, it's not a big deal. Do you guys have any special plans for tonight?"

"Dinner and a movie. You know, the usual. You know Ryan, he likes to keep things simple."

I giggled. "Sounds wonderful. Simple is good. Say hi to Ryan for me."

"Will do. What about you? Do you have any special plans?"

Without giving it much thought, my excitement got the better of me. I blurted everything out. I told her about what Justine had told me the night of the book club, and about all the questions Jim had asked. Then, while she was still quiet, I took a deep breath. "Okay, don't laugh, but I think tonight may be the night that Jim asks me to marry him."

The phone was silent as I waited for Cara's response. I was wondering if we'd gotten cut off when I heard her clear her throat.

"Whoa, Bailey, are you sure you're ready for that?"

Even though I could hear the concern in her voice, I felt myself getting defensive. "What do you mean? Am I ready?"

"How do I say this without sounding like an awful friend?"

"You just say it," I answered. "Now, what did you mean by that?"

"God, this is going to sound awful. Bailey, I never thought that you would get over Jackson. I mean, every time I think of you, I think of the two of you together."

"Why would you think of the two of us together?"

"I just hoped that time would heal things, and you'd eventually find your way back to him. I guess I always envisioned us marrying our high school sweethearts."

Closing my eyes for a moment, I took a minute to inhale deeply. It had taken me a long time to move on, many nights of tears and wishing things had of been different.

"Cara, it's been five years. It's been two years since I started dating Jim. This is the natural progression: date, get engaged, get married, perhaps have kids. Things weren't going that way with Jackson and I."

"Of course, you're right, it is the natural progression. I just thought that after all you'd been through with losing your brother and then with Jackson, you would have given it more time. Make sure that Jim really is the one."

"I have given it time, Cara, and I'm happy." I swallowed hard. Was I happy? I thought for a moment. I wasn't happy, but I knew if I told myself that enough, I'd finally start believing it. I just hoped that Cara didn't see through it.

"Happy? Are you? Are you really?"

I paused. She'd seen through it just like I knew she would. Sure, Jim and I had our problems. Okay, lots of problems, but they differed from the ones that Jackson and I had. We worked through them, or at least tried, which was more than what I could say about my previous relationship.

"Yes, I am," I said weakly.

"Okay. I just wish it sounded like you were," Cara said.

I should have been angry at her for not believing me, but from the sound of my voice, I wasn't even sure a stranger would believe me at this point. I looked down at the dress that lay beside me and then over at the towel, regret sinking in about what I'd spent.

"I'm happy." I repeated.

"Well, I guess that is all that matters. If you're happy, I'm happy." Cara replied.

"I am," I answered, perhaps a little too quickly. I was quiet for a moment. How did Cara do that? How did she see right through everything, and know I was as unsure of this as I was the day I walked away from my life back home? I pulled my feet up underneath me. How did she know I was constantly guessing whether this relationship was right for me, even after two years together? How did she know I was always wondering if I'd made the right decision by walking away from Jackson? I glanced at the clock and knew if I didn't get going, I was going to be late.

I also knew if I kept thinking about this, I'd call and cancel my date, as I'd done before, and drown my misery in a carb laden meal. "All right, you, I must get going. I am supposed to meet Jim at the restaurant at six."

"All right, well, happy anniversary, and I will call you tomorrow. Love you, bug."

"Love you too."

I took another drink of wine and placed the glass down on the table, tracing the rim with my finger. It was almost seven. I had been waiting for Jim for almost an hour. A loud gasp, followed by an excited scream, pulled my attention to the corner of the room. There I watched as a man kneeled down on the ground; a black velvet box perched in his hand as the woman across from him slipped the ring excitedly onto her finger. I smiled softly as I watched the couple embrace and then kiss before they sat back down.

"Hey, sorry I'm late." I felt a hand squeeze my shoulder.

I smiled as I looked up to see Jim standing there. Instead of kissing me, he walked over and pulled the chair out across from me and sat down. He looked exhausted; his hair was disheveled—a normal look from him running his fingers through after a stressful day. His suit jacket hung open, he'd already removed his tie, and he had already undone the first three buttons of his shirt. Suddenly, I felt very overdressed.

"It's okay." I shrugged, picking up my wineglass. "I had good company."

"I see that." He smiled, but it didn't quite reach his eyes.

I grabbed the bottle and poured another glass. "You really should try this wine before I finish the entire bottle."

"I'm good. It's been a long day. Not in the mood for drinks tonight."

I frowned. This wasn't the normal Jim, and I was wondering what had caused the lack of enthusiasm in him. He ran his hand through his hair once again, shrugged out of his suit jacket, and picked up the menu that was sitting on the table in front of him. He had barely looked at it before closing it again and letting out a sigh.

"Is everything okay?" I could hear the concern in my voice as I looked into his tired eyes. The more I worried something wasn't right, the faster I could no longer feel the effects of the wine I'd drank. I placed my glass down on the table to give him my undivided attention in case he wanted to talk. However, one look at his expression told me he didn't want to talk. What it told me was he didn't really want to be here with me. I'd seen it before.

"Yeah, like I said, it was a long day."

I looked over at the menu and then back to Jim. "If you weren't feeling up to tonight, you could have called. I'd have understood. Instead, I could have just come over and made dinner for us at your place."

"Welcome to The Porter House. Could I take your order?" the server asked, approaching our table, interrupting us. He emptied the rest of the wine from the bottle into Jim's glass. I was about to ask if we could have a couple more minutes to give Jim time to look over the menu, but he surprised me by placing his order.

"Yes. I'll have the New York strip cooked rare. A double baked potato, garlic mushrooms and onions on the side," he murmured, closing the menu, and pulling his cell phone from his breast pocket.

"Great choice, and for you, miss?"

I sat there looking at the man who sat across from me, not sure what to say. We'd never been to this restaurant before. Come to think of it, that was why he wanted to come here, yet he knew exactly what to order and he'd barely even glanced at the menu.

"Miss?"

"I'll have the chicken."

I watched as Jim pulled his cell phone from his breast pocket and began typing away, waiting for an answer from whoever had sent him a text, and then he typed back.

"And for the side, miss?"

"Rice and steamed vegetables," I mumbled absent-mindedly as I watched a funny little smile settle on Jim's face at something he'd read.

"Very good. Would you like another bottle of wine?"

When I didn't answer, Jim glanced up at me, cleared his throat and nodded. "Please." Then he went right back to the conversation he was having on his phone.

I watched as the server walked away, and once she was out of earshot, I turned back to Jim. He sat there, his face in his phone, as if I weren't even here. I could feel the anxiety building in my chest. Something was wrong. My mind flooded with all kinds of questions, but I only asked one.

"I thought you said you've never been here before?"

"I haven't," he said, finishing up whatever he'd been typing, then slipping his phone back into his pocket.

"Then how did you know what to order?"

Jim squirmed in his seat, clearly uncomfortable with my question. He shook his head and averted his eyes, then pulled his phone from his pocket again and began typing.

"Are you going to answer me?" I demanded. "Or are you going to have this date with your phone?"

"Sorry, it's my boss." He said, holding up his phone. "And I studied the menu earlier today, between meetings," he mumbled.

I looked down at the place setting in front of me, not sure what more to say. I took a sip of wine and looked back over at Jim, watching him type while I sat and waited for him to put his phone back in his pocket. Across the room, another couple's proposal caused excitement. I turned back to Jim, my smile quickly fading away when I saw he still had his cell phone in hand.

I sighed. "Am I keeping you from someone?" I questioned, annoyed.

Jim glanced up at me, at the annoyed look on my face, and quickly put his phone away just in time for our food to arrive. We both ate in unusual and uncomfortable silence as everyone around us enjoyed the company of their significant other.

Jim had just cleared his plate and set his fork down, stretched, and looked over at me. Clearing his throat, he leaned forward and rested his forearms on the table.

"I have something I want to talk to you about."

"Okay."

"You know, Bailey, we've been dating for what, two years now?"

I smiled and nodded before placing my fork down on the side of my plate. I had to turn my mood around. If it was his boss, he'd been texting with I knew it was something important. If he'd had a bad day, that wasn't his fault. I'd had plenty of those lately as well, and he never got upset with me.

"I've had a really great time with you. The places we've

traveled and seen together have been nothing short of amazing."

"Yes, they have." I smiled, thinking back through the adventures we'd had. The last one took us to Cozumel for our second anniversary. I could feel the anticipation building as I sat there thinking back to those nights in Mexico. One night, we'd gone down to the beach and made love under the moonlight. It had been amazing to feel the warm sea air caress my skin, and I wondered if tonight we'd be sharing the same feelings, of course, without the beach.

"I want you to know I really care about you."

"Of course, and I care about you too," I said in a serious tone, as I rested my hand in the middle of the table. "I love you."

Jim grabbed my hand. I could barely contain the butterflies in my stomach as he rubbed his thumb across the back of my hand. "Bailey, it's really been wonderful."

"Yes, it has," I said, meeting his eyes. Perhaps I'd mistaken his expression for a bad mood when he was just nervous.

His eyes dropped from mine and a look I didn't recognize came over his face. "Lately, though, I feel that something is missing between us."

"Missing?" I frowned, swallowing hard, wondering what he was talking about.

"Yes. I've given it lots of thought and I've searched

within myself, but I feel the connection I once felt to you is gone."

I frowned, trying to figure out where this was coming from. Everything in our relationship was the same. Nothing had changed. I had gone through a hard time a few weeks ago when I'd lost my job, and sure our relationship wasn't always roses, but then who's was.

"Bailey, I don't want to lead you on. That wouldn't be fair. I just don't feel this relationship is going anywhere. My feelings toward you, and us, have changed."

I could just imagine the look of shock on my face. Here I was expecting a proposal and, well, instead, I was getting dumped on our anniversary.

"What?" I asked a little louder than I should have, shock filling my voice.

"Bailey, I can't keep this up between us anymore. I just don't feel the same way about us anymore, and I haven't for quite some time. It's not right to lead you on, making you believe everything is fine."

My stomach turned, and I swallowed hard, fighting the burning sensation in my eyes from the tears that threatened to fall. I could feel eyes on me from every corner of the room as the patrons of the restaurant watched as my life shattered once again. I ripped my hand away from his, picked up my wineglass, and downed the contents as Jim sat and watched me.

"Bailey, that's not the only thing."

"I bet it's not." I murmured, still not believing what I'd heard.

"I've met someone else."

"What?" I questioned, slamming the glass down on the table.

"Perhaps this was the wrong spot to do this," he muttered under his breath as he looked around, noticing that people were now watching us.

"Perhaps this was the wrong spot to do this? Perhaps? Are you fucking kidding me? It's our anniversary. You are supposed to be proposing to me tonight. Not taking me out to dinner to break my heart, you asshole." I said through tightly clenched teeth.

Jim sat back and ran his hand over his face. "Proposing?" His eyes met mine. "Bailey, what are you talking about? What on earth would have given you that idea?"

I shrugged as Jim looked down at the table and then back at me.

"Justine." I murmured. "She saw you shopping downtown, said you were picking out rings? The joke must have been on me. Did you ask me all those questions about rings and vacation spots to buy a ring and propose to this other person?"

"No, no, no. God, Bailey, I was there helping my brother. She must have seen me when he stepped away to take a call. He asked me to get your insight because he was going to ask Sarah to marry him on their vacation."

"I see." I said, fighting back tears. "God, Jim, I thought things between us were more serious than this."

"Bailey, I'm so sorry. I don't know what else to say."

I could feel the burning behind my eyes and knew that tears weren't very far, and before they started pouring, I needed to get out of this restaurant. "Good night, that's what I'm going to say," I said, standing and grabbing my clutch purse from the table.

"Bailey, I don't think you should leave. Let me at least take you home. You've had a lot of wine. It's not safe for you to drive." Jim stood up and grabbed my arm.

I stopped and turned to look at him when I heard his phone ring. He held his finger up and pulled his phone from his pocket and checked the screen, then began typing away.

I let out a loud huff. "Yeah, I've had a lot of wine, and I can see you are busy. Don't worry, I'll make sure a cab takes me home. You obviously have more important things to take care of." I said, looking at the phone. "Even in the middle of a breakup, you can't leave that fucking phone alone."

I left Jim sitting at the table and rushed out of the restaurant, fighting tears all the way.

The ringing phone woke me from a dead sleep. I lifted my head, a sharp pain passing through my temples. I dropped my head back down onto my pillow; and rubbed my eyes with my fists blinking hard. The brightness in the bedroom giving me an even bigger headache than what I already had. Why didn't I pull the blinds?

I lay there trying to remember how I had gotten home. Had I taken a cab? Did Jim drop me off? Did I, oh god, had I driven? I went to roll over but felt restricted. Then I looked down at myself. The new dress I'd bought was wrapped tightly around me. No doubt it was all stretched to hell now. I let out a breath. My God, I had even fallen asleep with my clothes on. A loud ring went off again, and I reached over my head to grab the phone.

"Hello," I said groggily.

"Hello, my engaged twin."

"Engaged twin?" I questioned, rubbing my eyes.

"Yes! You weren't the only one who committed to forever last night. Ryan asked me to marry him last night too!" a cheerful Cara sang into the phone. "The wedding will be in December, and I want you to be my maid of honor. Of course, I'll return the favor!" she squealed. I could hear Ryan mumble something in the background, but couldn't make out what it was.

I felt my stomach turn. It was those words that brought me back to why I was such a mess this morning.

As if the breakup with Jim wasn't enough, now I would have to face watching Cara and Ryan get married.

"Congratulations." I sniffled, trying hard to be happy for my best friend. I knew I wasn't kidding anyone. I sounded like shit, and happiness and excitement were the furthest emotion from my voice.

"Bailey?"

"Yeah?" I said through a tight throat, trying to stifle the heavy sobs I knew were coming.

"What is it? What happened?"

"How do you know something happened?" I said, my eyes now tear filled.

"Bailey?" Her voice was softer this time. "What happened?"

I let out a deep breath and wiped the tears from my eyes. "Oh, Jim and I broke up last night." I sniffled. "He met someone else."

"That dirty rat bastard. Where is he? I will kill him. Don't hide him from me either, Bailey. I will find him and make sure he never uses his dick for anything ever again."

Even though I felt awful, I couldn't help but laugh through my tears at how protective Cara had always been. She'd been that way with Jackson in the beginning, too. "It's okay, you don't need to go all psycho. Our relationship - well, it just wasn't meant to be. It comes as some sort of shock, though, after thinking that I would have an entirely different conversation with you this morning."

"I'm sure. So what are you going to do now?"

"Honestly, I don't really know. Find work, I guess. Figure out where life is going to take me now. Pick up the pieces."

The line went quiet for a couple of minutes, and I could hear Cara whispering on the other end. I knew immediately she was probably telling Ryan everything.

"Don't tell Ryan everything!" I exclaimed. "At least wait until I'm off the phone."

"I'm not. Listen, I have an idea."

"You do? That at least makes one of us. Dare I even ask?"

"I was just thinking you could always come home. We could really use help to plan the wedding, and maybe you could get a job here. I'm sure your mom would be so happy to have you home."

A wave of panic came over me as I thought about returning to Sunset Cove. I hadn't been back since the day I left five years ago. I hadn't even gone back for a visit. Mom had come to me. I liked my new life. Or I did until now.

"What do you say? It will be like old times. We can shop, visit our old stomping grounds, and you can help me plan one hell of a wedding. Come on, I can't do it without you."

"I don't know, Cara. I'm not sure I'm ready to

return." If there was one thing I was certain of, it was that I wasn't ready to revisit my past. Any part of it.

"It's because of Jackson, isn't it?"

"What is?"

"Why you're hesitating." Cara said, her voice quieter now.

"Listen, it's not about Jackson. It's about me. It's about the fact I haven't been back since the funeral. It's about my brother and the fact that they still haven't found the guy responsible for taking his life that night."

"Sure..."

I hated it when Cara did that. She knew I hadn't dealt well with my brother's death. I'd been in therapy since it happened. I had confronted a lot of things from that night, but it didn't mean that many of those memories and thoughts didn't rise. The one thing I hadn't confronted was how things had changed in my relationship with Jackson after it had happened. I hated to admit it, but Cara knew me better than I knew myself.

I glanced at my cell phone as it vibrated on the table. As Cara began going on about all the things I could do there while trying to convince me to return, I leaned forward and grabbed my phone.

Jim had sent me a text. I took a deep breath and opened his message. Tears formed in my eyes once again as I read the words. It was final. He had messaged me to let me know he was on his way over and would leave my items from his apartment in the lobby of my apartment building for me to pick up. Which meant that he must have packed them up over the past couple of weeks while I'd been in bed with the flu. Suddenly, I felt as if he had been planning this for some time and just hadn't found the time to tell me.

"...and honestly, trying to plan a wedding for a couple hundred people in only a few short months is going to be hard enough. That's why I need you here. I know with you by my side, it will go off like a hitch. What do you say? Will you come home and help me? Please?"

I hadn't been paying one bit of attention to anything she had said and really didn't have any clue what I was agreeing to. Yet the words still came out, "Yeah Cara, you can count on me. I guess I am coming home."

# Jackson

I pulled my truck into my driveway and glanced over at the passenger seat to see Zoe smiling back at me. "What are your thoughts about the situation?" she asked.

I hadn't heard a word she'd said because I had zoned out to a song on the radio on the drive home. I'd gone into The Crooked Judge for a beer after work, just to unwind a little. I hadn't been looking for anything. Now here I sat, wondering what the hell I had been thinking when I'd invited Zoe back to my place.

Zoe and I had been involved on and off for the past six months. When I say involved, I don't mean a relationship. I mean, she is the longest running bed buddy I'd had without a commitment since, well, since my life had done a complete three-sixty a few years earlier. Keeping Zoe at a distance was the easiest way for me to walk away when the time was near, and I felt that time might be now. The last couple of times we'd been together, she'd been hinting at wanting more. However, tonight, I was feeling weak. I'd watched her across the room, her body swaying to the music, and soon all I could think about was having her body underneath me. We'd had a couple of drinks together, shared a few words, a dance and then the next thing I knew, she was following me to my truck.

"Come, let's go inside," I said, trying to divert the fact that I hadn't heard a word she'd said.

She smiled and slipped her hand into mine, and we walked up the path to my doorway together. I'd just shoved the key into the lock when I felt Zoe press her body into me from behind, her small hands running around my sides, down the front of my pants. I felt my cock jump as she ran her hand over the bulge that had already begun forming in my pants on the ride home.

Pulling her into my arms, I kissed her hard, throwing the door open. Once inside, I pushed her up against the wall, holding her there with my body as I kissed her neck, my left hand grasping her ass as I shut the door and turned the lock.

She slid out of her skirt while I kicked my shoes off, then she wrapped her arms around my neck. "Let's go slow tonight, Jackson," she moaned in my ear.

I gripped her ass and hoisted her up, allowing her to wrap her long legs around my waist. I didn't want to go slow. It had been a long, stressful day, and tonight I wanted nothing but quick, rough, animalistic sex. I carried her to the bedroom, ripping her shirt off as we went, and threw her down on the bed. I pulled my shirt off over my head and allowed my eyes to wander over her body as she lay sprawled before me.

"Go slow, Jackson." She moaned again as she slid her hand into her panties and began rubbing herself. I gripped my cock while I watched as her other hand wander up to her breast, and she gently pinched her nipple through her bra. "I want you to make love to me." She whispered.

I bent down and pulled both cups of her bra down, grasping her breasts in my hands. She ran her hand through my hair and then reached her hand into my boxers to stroke me. I bent down farther, taking her perfectly shaped rosy bud between my teeth, biting down until I heard her gasp. There was going to be nothing slow or gentle about tonight. I already felt as if I could blow at any second. I grabbed the box of condoms that lay on my bedside table, pulling one from the box.

I pushed her hand off me, rolled the condom on, and gripped her panties, ripping the delicate lace away from her body. I kneeled on the bed, gripped her leg, resting it on my shoulder. I could tell from the look in her eyes she wanted me to take my time, and then she confirmed my thoughts.

"Please, go slow." She said again as she ran her fingers through my hair, resting her hand on the back of my neck.

Ignoring her, I gripped her hips; lined myself up and entered her in one swift movement. A harsh moan escaped her mouth. I didn't give her a second to get adjusted to me. Instead, I went right to it, pumping hard and relentlessly into her until she was begging to come. I slowed my pace, and within seconds of her release, I felt my own.

I collapsed on her, breathing hard, and then rolled off her, getting up to dispose of the condom. When I returned, I flopped down on the bed. I closed my eyes and was just about asleep when I felt the bed move. I glanced over to see her getting up, while murmuring something about leaving. She had already begun collecting her things. This was the usual scene for us, and I didn't feel it needed to change, so I dropped my head back onto the pillow and covered my eyes with my arm.

"I've got to get going. I left my car at the bar, so I'll need you to give me a lift."

Even though I wanted my bed to myself, I also didn't want to get up and take her anywhere. "Zoe, it's late. Just stay the night. I'll take you in the morning," I murmured.

She didn't answer, instead she let out a huff. Then I heard the bathroom door click shut and the water run. Staring up at the ceiling, I ran my hand over my face, wondering if I shouldn't just take her back to her car now. I could tell her things were over after I dropped her off and return home to get a good night's sleep. I was about to get up when I heard the bathroom door open; the light shut off, and the patter of her feet padding across the carpet towards the bed.

"Night."

Before I could protest, I felt her snuggle into my side and press a kiss to my cheek.

I could feel the trickle of sweat dripping down my back. The vest I wore was heavy. I was hot as I ran down the dark alley. My clothes were soaked, and I was out of breath. I would never reach the end of the alley. In the distance, I could see two men standing across from one another, both with their weapons aimed at one another. I could hear my partner yell, warning him once again to drop his weapon, then the shots rang out.

I picked up the pace, signaling to the others who ran behind me to hurry. My heart was beating through my chest when, in the distance, I saw my partner up ahead, now shielding himself behind a car. He stepped out, shots were fired again, only this time he went down. I could see his body now lying sprawled out on the concrete, lifeless.

I stopped, drew my gun from the holster, and eased

around the corner, checking for signs of the shooter, but he was already gone. I was just about to do another check when I heard the gurgled call for help.

I looked again to make sure it was clear, then I ran over to where my partner lay and dropped to the ground. I pulled my flashlight from my belt. "Connor, man, where you hit?" I questioned, looking over his vest for signs of damage.

"He's been hit!" I yelled out as Ryan and Dave came running over. Dave was already on the radio and an ambulance was on the way.

"Did you see who did it?" Ryan called, running up to us.

"They are on their way, man, hold on," I pleaded with Connor.

I put my hand on Connor's back to comfort him, and that was when I felt the warm, thick wetness of blood. He'd been shot just under his arm. The shot had missed his vest. I flashed my light around on the ground, noticing a lot of blood. "There's got to be more than one wound, guys." I mumbled, flashing the light on the ground again. I noticed his pants were also soaked. He'd not only been shot in the upper torso area, but another bullet had hit him somewhere in the leg.

"Can't breathe..." he whispered, gripping my arm as blood trickled out the side of his mouth. Panic filled me as I wondered if they had hit him in the lungs.

"How far away is the ambulance?" Dave questioned over the radio.

"About ten minutes," the dispatcher radioed back.

I glanced down into the face of my partner. "Can't breathe..." he pleaded, pulling at my shirt.

"Guys, help me roll him onto his back. Let's try to make him a little more comfortable." Everything in me screamed not to do it. I knew we weren't supposed to move anyone for fear we would do more damage. Yet as he pleaded with me, I also didn't want to watch my partner, and soon-to-be brother-in-law, die because he couldn't breathe. I cradled his shoulders, while Dave kneeled to help me swiftly roll him without moving him too much.

"Oh, fuck!" Ryan yelled and immediately dropped to his knees to put pressure on a gunshot wound on his leg that was now gushing blood at an alarming rate. Dave let go of his legs and helped Ryan apply pressure to the area. We knew we had to slow the bleeding.

"Connor, stay with us," I pleaded, pulling my belt off. I wrapped it around his upper leg, pulling it tight, hoping to help the guys stop the bleeding, but it did little good he was passing out.

"Look after Bailey, bro, please." His voice was weaker than it had been before and the pale color of his skin worried me.

"Come on, man, don't talk like that. You're going to be fine, just fine. Help is on the way." I looked up, trying to see if I could see the flashing lights of the ambulance. "Fuck, where is that ambulance?"

There was one more gurgled breath and then silence as his head fell to one side. The three of us looked at one another, and I dropped my head in defeat. When I finally found the strength to raise my head, both Dave and Ryan were gone. I was in the same dark alley. My heart rate increased as I stared down at Connor's cold, lifeless body.

"Dave? Ryan? Where is the fucking ambulance?" I mumbled, staring at Connor's lifeless body.

"Connor, Connor, wake up!" I yelled. "The ambulance is on its way. Come on, man." I screamed as loud as I could for help, but no one came. An eerie silence fell over me. I looked around and then back to my partner and watched in horror as Connor sat straight up, turned, and looked into my eyes. "You didn't do as I asked, Jackson. Why didn't you do as I asked?"

"I tried," I cried. "I tried so hard. She wouldn't let me help her."

Connor looked at me, more like right through me, and I froze. "Wake up. Wake up, Jackson." He said.

I closed my eyes tightly as I listened to the sounds of my strange surroundings, my heart beating hard. I felt someone shake me. I opened my eyes and looked around my bedroom. I was about to push them away when I realized it was Zoe who was beside me, gently shaking me.

"You all right? You were dreaming," she said, gripping my hand. "Who's Connor?"

I ran my hand over my clammy face and inhaled deeply, my mind wandering back to the look in Connor's eyes in my dream.

"Are you going to tell me who Connor is?" Zoe asked again.

Instead of answering her, I was silent. I rolled onto my side and sat up on the edge of the bed, trying to catch my breath. The words he spoke in my dream ran at the forefront of my mind. *You didn't do as I asked, Jackson. Why didn't you do as I asked?*

"Did you want to talk about it?" she questioned, placing her hands on my shoulders, massaging them.

"No," I barked, throwing the covers off me and climbing from the bed.

"It might help."

"It won't help. Just go to sleep," I bit out and grabbed my sweats from the bottom of the bed and slipped them on.

"Where are you going?"

"Outside for some fresh air. Go to sleep. I'll be back in a bit," I said, grabbing a T-shirt and throwing it over my head.

"Want some company?" she questioned.

"No. I just want to be alone. Go back to sleep," I mumbled and pulled the bedroom door shut.

I'd barely slept the rest of the night and was glad when I dropped Zoe off outside of The Crooked Judge. She had spent the morning asking me if I was okay, and no matter how many times I'd told her I was fine, she couldn't let it go. I remained tight-lipped, however, and just before she left my truck, that was when I dropped the news that I no longer wanted to see her. There was no doubt I'd upset her. The way she slammed the door to my truck and marched off across the parking lot without so much as even looking back at me told me so.

As I pulled out of the parking lot, I didn't give her another thought. I knew I wasn't ready to go home yet, so I drove across town and pulled into Ryan and Cara's driveway. I walked up the walkway and banged on the front door.

"Come in," I heard Ryan call. I stepped inside and could see Ryan in the kitchen making a sandwich. "Hey, man."

"Hey, what's going on? How did last night go?" I questioned, removing my shoes and throwing my jacket on the chair in the living room before making my way into the kitchen. I knew he'd been planning on proposing to

Cara and wondered if he actually had the balls to go through with it.

"She said yes," he said, holding his hands in the air as if he'd just scored a touchdown.

I chuckled. "That's outstanding, man, congrats. Was there really any doubt?" I pulled open the refrigerator and grabbed a coke, cracking the tab and downing the cold liquid. "I mean, it's been what, ten years?"

"Help yourself," Ryan said with his mouth full.

"Don't mind if I do," I said, grabbing a slice of lunch meat from the package on the counter and shoving it into my mouth, giving him a cocky grin. "So, what now?" I questioned.

"Well, I guess, now it's plan, plan, plan. I swear all I wanted was a little some-some last night, but she was busy pulling out planning boards. The ring hadn't even been on her finger for five hours. She's apparently already assembled her side of the wedding party."

I laughed to myself and shook my head at Ryan. "Buddy, I told you."

"You told him what?" Cara asked, coming into the kitchen, a laundry basket resting on her hip.

"He told me nothing." Ryan blurted out. "Look who stopped by."

"I see who stopped by. Good morning, Jackson," she said, leaning in to give me a hug and a kiss on the cheek.

"Good morning, Cara. Congratulations."

"Thanks. It's going to be so amazing," she said. "I've already got my girls ready."

"That's exactly what Ryan just told me," I said, winking in Ryan's direction.

"Of course, you will be Ryan's best man, right?" Cara questioned. "He's been having a hard time coming up with names of people for his side. I'm sure that you can help him with a list, right?"

I chuckled to myself. "Can I help him with the list? The best man part, that depends." I shrugged.

"On?"

"On what kind of monkey suit you're going to want us all to wear, and how much you are prepared to bribe me to stand up for this fucker?" I said, chuckling, looking over at Ryan, who was now shooting me daggers. I loved getting under his skin.

"We haven't gotten to that part just yet, but I should have that figured out in the next couple of weeks." Cara said.

"Can I let you know then?" I laughed just as the phone rang.

Cara shook her head and smiled at me while Ryan answered.

"Cara, phone," Ryan said, holding the phone out for her to take.

"I'll mark you down and make sure your suit has an extra side of monkey." She winked as she turned and smiled at Ryan before heading down the hall with the phone in her hand.

"Now that's settled. Are we going to watch the game tonight? We can kick back at my place."

"Yeah, that should be fine. Specter coming?"

"I think so. At least, that was the plan. I'll order pizza and wings, and grab the beers, so be there by kickoff?"

"Sounds good."

"I'll see if Cameron wants to join us, too." I murmured.

Ryan nodded just as Cara walked into the kitchen, threw the phone on the base, and turned to Ryan and me with a great big grin on her face.

"Before you give me a to-do list, I'm heading to Jackson's tonight for the game," Ryan said, glancing over at me.

"That's fine."

"You mean you aren't angry that I won't be home?"

"No, nothing could make me angry. I'm so excited. Everything is finally coming together and...Bailey is coming back. That was her on the phone. She just confirmed that she is going to be my maid of honor."

I swear it was those very words that stopped my heart in its tracks.

Cara turned and smiled at me as if she had announced they were having lasagna for dinner and continued on her way down to the basement with the laundry. Ryan looked over at me, his mouth full and concern lining his face. He was waiting until Cara was out of earshot, then leaned forward.

"Man, you all right?" he questioned.

I tore my eyes away from where Cara had stood as the shock of what she had said ran through my mind. I slowly nodded. "Why wouldn't I be?"

Ryan met my eyes and shrugged. "Oh, I don't know. Hearing that the girl who broke your heart is returning home can sometimes do a thing to a guy."

"She didn't break my heart." I replied, looking away. Hearing her name had felt like a kick in the gut.

"Really? That's not how I remember it, Jackson."

I looked down at the can in my hand, not sure how I felt. "Yep, you're right, but I'm good."

# Bailey

My mother had done nothing to my room since I'd been gone. It was still the same pale pink color that I had chosen when I was in my early teens. If I were going to stay here and I wasn't going to get a place of my own, then this room would need a do-over. I stretched, yawned, and rolled onto my back, laying in bed listening to the birds chirping outside my open window. It had been a sound I'd missed while living in a high-rise in a heavily populated city for the past five years. I'd been back in Sunset Cove for exactly forty-eight hours, and it had felt as if I'd never left.

I kicked the purple comforter off me and placed my feet down on the bright pink plush carpet. God, why did I choose pink? I thought to myself. God, I hated pink. I looked around at the mess of my belongings on the floor and then over at the desk. There, facing the wall, was a picture frame I hadn't noticed until now. I picked it up and flipped it in my hands, looking down at it. Jackson sat behind me; his arms wrapped around me. My hands rested on his forearms and we both smiled at the camera. I remembered the day we'd taken this picture. We'd hiked up to the ridge and had a picnic lunch. Then we'd spent the afternoon laying on the picnic blanket, talking and dreaming of our future together.

I sighed. Suddenly, I started thinking of everything that had happened shortly after and I shoved the frame into the desk drawer. I took a moment to gather myself, then reached for a bag on the floor. Everywhere I looked, there were reminders of him and me. The teddy bear he had won for me at the Sunset Cove Fair sat on the chair in the corner of my room. Ticket stubs from one of the last concerts we had been to were stuck in the mirror's frame that hung on the wall. The necklace he had given me for our sixth anniversary lay perfectly sprawled out on top of my dresser, so the chain didn't tangle. Memories of him were everywhere.

"Time to rise and shine," I heard my mother call from the hall. "You start your new job today. Don't want you to be late."

I smiled to myself. It didn't matter how long I'd been gone from home, Mom always thought I needed a guiding hand. I reached for my sweatshirt that hung over the footboard of the bed and threw it over my head. Trudging to the bathroom, I swept my hair up into a ponytail and splashed some water on my face before heading to the kitchen.

The smell of freshly brewed coffee and pancakes greeted me. "Morning, Mom."

"Good morning," she said as she bent into the fridge and pulled out the syrup. "Did you want juice? I have orange and apple."

"Nah, I'm good with coffee. Not much of a juice drinker."

"Bailey, you really should have juice. A good balanced diet contains Vitamin C in the morning."

"I have Vitamin C right here." I said, holding up my cup of coffee and grinning.

Mom gave me a look and shook her head while placing the bottle of juice in the center of the table.

I grabbed a juice glass from the cupboard and set it on the table, then took my favorite mug and filled it, carefully placing the carafe back on the hot plate. I took a sip of the hot coffee and looked out the kitchen window into the backyard. Four hooded orioles sat on the edge of the birdbath, each one taking their turn in the water.

"So, what's it like to be back home?"

"A little surreal, but nice. I see you're still feeding the orioles."

"Yes, Connor used to love them. He would watch

them for hours on end when he was younger. They seem to be here in abundance ever since..." She stopped talking.

I turned to see her standing there, her eyes closed, her hand wrapped around the handle of the flipper tight enough to make her knuckles turn white.

"I mean, for the last few years," Mom murmured as she flipped the pancakes onto a plate.

I swallowed hard as I took on her moment of unease and sadness to invade me. I looked out the back window, at the trees that had changed color, brilliant yellow and the slightest hint of orange stood out in the sunlight. Even though I knew mom was okay, I couldn't imagine how she must be feeling. I missed my brother so much, but I had gotten to escape the nightmare. Mom, however, still lived in the same house she was in the night Dad walked out on us, and the unfortunate night that asshole had taken Connor from us.

I took a deep breath, turned around, and sat down at the table, sipping on my coffee, watching as Mom dumped another dollop of batter into the pan.

"So, you've been out and about a lot since you came home. Been doing anything interesting?" She questioned.

Guilt invaded me. "Yeah, I know, and I'm sorry about that. I promise it won't keep up. After I had to go for my interview, I needed to get a few things. Cara wanted to have dinner, and I had to change my address on my driver's license, but soon I'll be around all the time, and you will beg me to go out."

"Nonsense. That would never happen. I've missed having you home."

Sipping my coffee, I checked my phone for any messages. I was reading an email from Justine when Mom's spoke, causing me to jump.

"Mrs. Fisher said she saw you downtown the other day."

"Oh?" I swallowed hard. "How is she? I haven't seen her in ages."

"She's good. When Bill died, she had a hard time, but I got her into the support group I joined after Connor passed. She told me she saw you downtown, near the Sunset Cove Police Department."

I looked down at the floor and closed my eyes for a second, then cleared my throat. "Yeah, so what?" I knew what my mother was hinting at. I could tell by the sound of her voice.

"Oh, nothing. I just thought it was strange you were all the way downtown."

I looked at my mother, knowing full well what was coming. "Mom, just ask me what you want to know. You want to know if my being down there had something to do with Jackson?"

"Well, now that you mention it, I guess I was wondering if you went to see him?"

"Mom don't do this," I begged, letting out a huff. It was too soon to mention him to me.

"Do what, baby girl? It's an honest question."

"Do this! Exactly what you are doing. Jackson and I are over, and we've been over for five years. There is no more us, nor will there be any more of us."

"Bailey, I just figured you would want to see him. I mean, it's been a long time." She set the plate of pancakes down in front of me along with the syrup, then looked at me. "Honey, I think it's time you at least speak to him. He was your brother's partner as well."

"No, Mom, it isn't time I speak to him. I closed that chapter on my life a long time ago. Please, respect that." I picked up the bottle of syrup and drowned the hot pancakes in the sticky syrup.

"Bailey, I do respect that. Don't think that I don't." She said, turning back to the stove. "I just thought it would be good for you both to sit down and talk, like adults."

I looked down at the pile of food in front of me, suddenly losing my appetite. I was so lost in thought that I'd barely noticed she'd flipped the last pancake onto her plate and sat down across from me.

"Bailey, I'd have thought you'd already have sunk your fork into that fluffy stack of pancakes you coated in syrup already. Aren't you going to eat?" she questioned, grabbing the bottle of syrup and lightly coating hers.

I shook my head. "No, I've suddenly lost my appetite." I got up from the table and placed my partially full mug on the counter, and walked out of the kitchen.

"Bailey, you need to eat. You work today." Mom yelled.

"I'll grab something there." I shouted and then stopped in the hall, pinching the bridge of my nose. I took a breath and then turned around and stepped back into the kitchen. "...and, just so you know, if you're expecting Jackson and I to get back together, you can forget it. We are over. You can tell that to Mrs. Fisher, too."

"Order is for table ten, Bailey!" Glenn yelled in my direction from where he was pouring a couple of beers for two men sitting at the bar.

I nodded and slid the tray of drinks onto the palm of my hand, carefully balancing it. I turned and began walking toward table ten when I caught eyes with Dave Specter. He and Ryan were seated in my section. I dropped the drinks off at table ten, quickly taking their food order, and then made my way over to the two men.

"Well, Bailey Scott, as I live and breathe," Dave said,

flashing me that sexy smile every woman in Sunset Cove loved.

"Hey, Dave, Ryan, how are you?"

"Good, love. Nice to see your pretty face back here. I wasn't sure I'd ever see you again," Dave said.

"Thanks. It's a little surreal being back here, but it's good to be back with Mom. What can I get for you guys tonight?"

"Whatever is on tap," they both said in unison.

I let out a laugh. "Okay." I smiled and was about to turn away when Dave cleared his throat.

"So, when did you get back to town?"

"About fifty-eight hours ago now."

"I see you're counting." Dave chuckled.

"No. I'm settling in. I couldn't say no. My best friend practically begged me to come back to help with some wedding plans," I answered, glancing at Ryan, who smiled at me.

"Yeah, Ryan mentioned you might be returning for the wedding," he said, looking in Ryan's direction. "How's your mom been? I haven't seen her in a while."

"She's good. She's been busy with her gardening club, but she is glad to have me back home. Is it just going to be the two of you tonight?" I questioned, trying to calm the butterflies in my stomach at the thought of Jackson possibly joining them.

"Yeah, it's just us," Ryan answered. "You don't need to worry." He winked.

"All right, two of whatever is on tap, coming up!" I said as I threw two coasters down on the table.

I was halfway back to the bar when the door opened and three gang members from the Green Cobras walked in. Things apparently hadn't changed around here, I thought to myself. These guys had always frequented The Crooked Judge. The three of them stopped just inside the door and looked around. One of them looked in my direction and looked longingly at me. Chills ran through me as his eyes ran the length of my body before meeting my eyes again. I'd hoped that Dave and the rest of the Sunset Cove Police had run them out of the area after Connor's death, but it appeared they hadn't. There had been a lot of speculation that it had been one member Connor had crossed that night. Yet, no one could be sure since there hadn't been a clear sighting. Regardless, I swallowed hard and put it to the back of my mind that one of these very men could be the one responsible for my brother's death. As I walked by them on my way to the bar, I heard one of them give a low whistle. I ignored them and went about my business until the three of them came over to the bar and took a seat right next to me.

I could feel his eyes on me. Hell, I could almost feel his breath, too.

"Well, well, what do we have here?" he said, running his finger along my arm.

My eyes fell to where his tatted fingers rubbed my arm. The letters GREE were visible, and then I looked at the snake on his forearm.

"I'm Garrick. This is Linden and Dorian. What's your name, beautiful? Not seen you around these parts before. Are you new around these parts?"

When I didn't immediately answer him, he chuckled. "That's okay. We like shy girls, don't we, guys? They are much more fun." He said, running his forefinger over my forearm once again.

A chill ran through me, and I was about to say something when Glenn turned around and glared at the three of them. "Gentlemen, I've told you before, you can come in here, play pool, drink, and eat, but don't bother my staff. Now what can I get for you?" he asked, not faltering once while he placed the beers on my tray and nodded for me to get out of there.

I rushed to the table where Dave and Ryan sat and set the beers down in front of them. "Here you go, guys. Did you want anything to eat?"

"Nah, we're good right now." Dave smiled at me and raised his glass before taking a sip.

"So, have you seen Jackson since you been back?" Ryan asked me outright as he, too, took a sip of his beer.

I looked at Dave and noticed he was giving Ryan the eye.

"What?" Ryan questioned, looking over at Dave. "Someone's got to ask her," he mumbled like I wasn't even standing there.

"Cara is going to have your balls, you know that, right?" Dave questioned, looking over at me and giving me a wink.

I smirked and cleared my throat. "Just so you know, Ryan, no, I haven't seen him. You can let Cara know that, too."

A loud bang behind me caused to me to jump, and I turned in time to see a pool cue being thrown to the ground by one of the gang members.

"Fuckin assholes," Dave mumbled.

"Tell me about it," I said, looking in their direction.

"You make sure you steer clear of those guys, Bailey." Dave said, nodding in their direction.

I nodded. "Have there been any updates on my brother's case? Mom won't tell me," I questioned, looking at Dave. I knew this wasn't the time or place to ask, but curiosity was getting the best of me. I needed to know the truth.

"We have a couple of suspects. Nothing solid."

"You don't think it's one of these..." I swallowed hard, my throat getting tight at the thought.

"Bailey, don't you worry. We are still working on it,

okay? Just ignore the fact that these guys are even in here, and if they cause any trouble, call the station."

I nodded, looking at the ground. "Will do." I glanced around and noticed I was being flagged to a couple of tables. "I've got to go. Enjoy your drinks."

The night went on, Ryan and Dave left and two hours later, the only patrons in the bar were the three Green Cobras members and two other tables of two. It was then that three other men walked in that I didn't recognize. Glenn was in the back doing the order, and I was minding the bar. I watched as the three men walked over to where Garrick, Linden, and Dorian were playing pool. They exchanged words between them, and I watched out of the corner of my eye as I wiped down the bar. They looked at one another, and then one of them placed a pile of cash on the edge of the pool table and they racked a set of new balls.

I knew Glenn wasn't a fan of the Green Cobras being in here, never mind them betting in his bar, but he said nothing to them. I did as Dave said and continued on with my job, pouring drinks and waiting on the two tables that were here. Once I'd delivered drinks to everyone, I began loading glasses into the dishwasher. I watched the game going on over in the corner. The three men I'd never seen before cheated their way to winning, only I wasn't the only one who had seen it. Garrick had seen it, too.

As one man threw it in their face, he picked up the

money. Garrick grabbed the other by the throat and shoved him up against the wall. The force of him hitting the wall caused me to drop a glass to the floor, shattering it.

"Fuck," I whispered under my breath, afraid that the shatter of glass would turn their attention to me, but none of them noticed.

"You cheated, you fucker?" Garrick hissed, reaching around, and pulling a knife from his belt, holding it up to the guy's throat. Linden and Dorian pulled their knives too and approached the other two men, completely ignoring the fact that they were in the presence of other people.

I didn't wait another minute for this to move ahead any further. Instead, I stepped into the back room and dialed the police.

# Jackson

The first half of my shift had been uneventful. I was making my way back to the station to catch up on some paperwork and grab a bite to eat when a call came over the radio. There was a problem at The Crooked Judge, and they were requesting police backup. It was an odd call for a weeknight. Normally, the place was full of couples having dinner. I radioed the station, letting them know I was on my way over to the bar.

I'd just pulled up outside the bar when Greg and Matt brought two men I recognized as members of the Green Cobras. Both men were in cuffs, and Matt and Greg took them over and placed them in the back of their cruiser.

"Gentlemen, what happened?" I asked as I climbed out of my car and approached them. I glanced into the back of their cruiser and recognized Dorian Patten and Linden Becker.

"Pool game gone bad. There were apparently three Cobra members here, but the one who started it all took off just as we arrived. Almost knocked Matt over on our way in. These two were still inside, causing shit."

"You alright, Matt?"

"I'll be fine. I didn't even know what hit me."

"Did you get a look at him or a name from these two?"

"No, these two aren't talking," Greg answered.

I nodded, looking over my shoulder in both directions. The street was quiet, and there wasn't anyone to be seen in either direction. It looked like a normal Wednesday night.

"What about the other guys, the ones they fought with?"

"They are inside, sitting at the bar. These two roughed them up a little, pulled knives on them for cheating."

"All right, so you taking these two in? Did you get statements?"

"We are taking them in, but we didn't get statements. The bartender who saw it all had gone for a break when we got there. I guess she was a little rattled, being new in the area, so we are waiting for her to return."

I frowned. I'd just been here two nights ago. There wasn't a new bartender. "New employee?" I questioned.

"Yeah, apparently her first night on the job." Greg chuckled.

"All right, well, if you two want to take these two in, I can go in, talk to the guys they fought with. I'll also get a statement from the bartender and any other witnesses there may have been."

"Matt can take them in. I'll stay and give you a hand," Greg said, heading back toward the door.

"Sounds good."

Matt got into his car and drove off toward the station while we headed into the bar. While Greg went to talk to the three men who had been involved, I walked around the bar talking to the other customers to see if they had witnessed anything. I sat down at every table and took down notes as each person provided me statements of their version of what had happened. It all seemed to be started by the one guy who got away.

When I finished, I walked up to the bar. Glenn stood there, rag slung over his shoulder, and smiled. "Hey, Jackson, thanks for coming." He extended his hand out, and we quickly shook.

"No problem. I see these guys are still causing shit in here."

"No. They've been good since I laid down the ground rules. Not sure what happened tonight, I was in the back when it all happened." Glenn said, nodding toward the three guys that Greg was still speaking with.

"Okay, I don't recognize them from around here."

"Me neither."

"I was told that the bartender who called the police was on her break when my guys got here. Is she back yet? We'd really like to get a statement from her before we leave, especially now that we know one of them ran off."

"She should be back in a moment. She was pretty rattled, so I gave her a little extra time. The Cobras haven't been here in months, and the first night they are, this happens. They are going to have to stop coming in here, Jackson. This place is going to get a bad rap if they don't."

"Do you know which one of them ran off? Did you see him at all?"

"Yeah, the big guy, Garrick. He'd come in with them tonight. You'd know him, I'm sure."

"I know of him, yes."

"Well, the second he heard the sirens, he apparently ran out the door. I wouldn't doubt if he isn't the one who started it all, but then I was in the back, so I can't say for sure."

"How long had they been here?"

"Came in around six, I'd say. They ordered a few drinks, tried to hit on my new bartender and server, but you know how they are. These other guys, though, I have no clue who they are," Glenn said, nodding toward the other three men who had been involved.

I nodded and then heard a door slam in the distance,

and Glenn held his finger up and poked his head around the entrance to the back.

"Good, you're back. The police want a word with you."

"Be right there," I heard a familiar voice say.

"She'll be out in a minute." Glenn went back to straightening up and clearing dishes off tables, and I turned around to see Greg make his way back over to me. "Just about ready to head out?" he asked as he put his notebook in his back pocket.

"Yeah, just waiting to talk to the bartender who called the police."

"I don't know about you, but I'm convinced it was the one who ran who started it all."

I nodded. "Yeah, that was what the others said as well. We'll wait and see what this bartender has to say and go from there. Those guys really should come down to the station, anyway. You should let them know that."

"Already did. They said they'd meet us down there."

"I'm sorry, you wanted to talk to me, officer?" a quiet voice asked behind me, and I turned around and met a face I'd thought I'd never see again.

It was as if all the air had left the room. The second my eyes landed on that dirty blonde hair, and those soft, dreamy blue eyes, I was done. My eyes skimmed down her sexy body, a body I'd once had in my bed, and I swallowed hard. I cleared my throat and fought the sensation that ran through my body, reminding me just how attracted I'd been to her.

"Bailey?" That was the only word I could get out of my mouth, as once again, my eyes ran the length of her body before returning to look into her eyes.

"Jackson," she murmured, staring back at me.

"What are you..." I stopped mid-sentence, lost in her eyes. I didn't need to ask. I knew she had moved back here. I just didn't think I'd run into her this soon.

The sound of my name falling off her lips sent a wave of heat through my body. We stood in silence, staring at one another, and in those few moments, I had completely forgotten what it was I was even doing here and what I'd even wanted to see her for.

Greg cleared his throat and stepped in. "Miss," he said, looking up at me and frowning. "we wanted to have a few words about what took place here tonight. I understand you were the one who called the police after the fight broke out. If you have a few minutes, we have a few questions we'd like to ask you."

Her eyes never left mine as Greg continued speaking. Bailey stood there nodding at everything Greg said, but I doubted she was even listening. She confirmed my suspicions when he asked his first question. Instead of answering the question, she only nodded. Greg repeated the question once again, this time a little louder. She jumped at the sound of his voice, but finally, her eyes left mine and she slowly began answering what he wanted to know.

"Now, a little on the personal side. We were told by Glenn that the one man who left earlier had put his hands on you. Are you able to provide us a description of him?"

I met her eyes and clenched my fists at my side. The thought of another man putting his hands on her in any way boiled my blood.

She didn't say anything, but when her eyes met mine, I knew what had happened earlier had her rattled.

"Bailey, if you can't remember exactly what he looked like, it's okay. Anything that may help identify him would be helpful."

"Ummm...he had a snake tattoo. Wrapped around his forearm and letters." She closed her eyes and brought her fingers up to her temples, rubbing them. "GREE, were on his fingers."

"Okay. Thanks, miss, that will be all for now. If we have any more questions, we will be in touch." Greg said, pocketing his notebook.

I hadn't taken my eyes off her until I felt Greg pull me by the arm. I lifted my hand to wave goodbye to Bailey and followed him outside. As soon as the cool, fresh air finally hit me in the face, it was like I woke up.

"What the hell happened to you in there?" Greg asked as we stopped just beside my car.

"What do you mean?" I questioned, swallowing hard.

"Come on Jackson, you obviously know her. Some sort of history between you?"

Greg was new to Sunset Cove and did not know about the history between Bailey and me. However, Dave knew, and once he found out that I hadn't kept my head about me, he'd pull me off this case faster than I could blink.

"Let's not talk about it! It's in the past, all right."

"Didn't seem that way." He shrugged. "It seemed like it had just happened and there were a lot of things left unsaid between the two of you."

Ignoring his comment, I walked around to the driver's side door and ripped it open. Climbing in, I pulled the door shut, shoved the key in the ignition, and started the car.

"Are you planning on walking back to the station?" I yelled as I rolled down the passenger's side window.

"No."

"Then get in," I barked as Greg pulled the door open and climbed in. The door had barely closed when I pulled away from the curb, taking off toward the station and in the opposite direction of Bailey Scott.

# Bailey

I'd gotten home later than I'd planned from my first night at work. I'd never been so thankful that Mom wasn't sitting in the living room chair waiting up for me like she used to do.

I hadn't been able to forget about him after seeing him tonight. My entire way home, all I wanted to do was to revisit old memories. When I got home, I cracked a bottle of wine and sat cross-legged on the floor of my bedroom. I held my picture album in my lap, flipping through years of memories with tears in my eyes. Pictures of us when we were younger, prom pictures, pictures of the camping trips that Jackson, Connor, and I had gone on during the summers. I revisited the swearing-in ceremony all the police officers go through. Both Connor and Jackson looked so handsome in their uniforms as they took their oaths.

A couple hours passed and the bottle of wine I'd opened was gone. I flipped the next few pages and now I was looking at some sort of alternate universe—the year after my brother had died. Tears ran down my face as I looked at the picture of Jackson and I. Then, finally, I flipped to the very last picture we'd ever taken together, and that was when I lost it. I sobbed as the tears streamed down my face. I closed the book and climbed into bed and cried myself to sleep just like I had done for the first two years after I'd moved away.

A heavy feeling surrounded me this morning. I'd barely gotten three hours' sleep after my trip down memory lane, and I was paying for it this morning. My head ached. I approached The Blessed Bean, took a deep breath, and pulled the door open. The familiar surroundings of my favorite coffee shop put a smile on my face. It was the first time I had been there since I had returned to Sunset Cove.

I glanced around the room and saw Cara sitting in a corner booth waving frantically at me. I lifted my hand in a wave and began approaching the table when she jumped out of her seat and wrapped her arms around me.

"Been in town almost four days and you haven't even come to see me yet. It's about time you got here," she said as she squeezed me tightly to her.

"Sorry, it's been...an adjustment. Just don't tell my mom you didn't see me until today. I told her we had dinner the other night. Now sorry I'm late, I had to stop at the pharmacy and pick up Mom's prescription. There was a line," I said, shrugging.

"Your secret is safe with me and forget about it. You're here now. I ordered our coffees, but I didn't order any food because I didn't know what you would want. They have fresh pumpkin spice muffins, apple cookies, and cinnamon sugar scones."

"Ooh, those scones sound like something to die for, but then I haven't had one of those muffins since I left. Let's get those," I said, laughing and grabbing my wallet.

"No way, put that wallet away. You moved all the way back here for me. The least I can do is buy you a muffin and coffee," Cara said, nodding to my wallet. She grabbed hers instead and headed to the counter. Seconds later, she returned with two pumpkin spice muffins.

I took a bite and closed my eyes, savoring the flavor.

"Good, huh?" Cara asked, taking a bite of hers.

"So good!" I murmured, taking another bite.

"So, I heard about what happened last night at The Crooked Judge. Are you okay?"

"Yeah, I'm fine. It was baffling how fast things escalated. Those guys rattled me pretty good, especially the ones who put his hands on me." I said, rubbing my temples, trying to calm the pounding in my head.

"You all right?"

"Yeah, just a headache is all. You don't have anything, do you?" I had figured it would calm itself, but now the pain was worse and I was afraid that combined with the bit of food I had in my stomach, I might be sick.

Cara dug through her purse, finally finding a container, and shook two headache tablets into her hand. "Here you go. Well, it was a good thing you called the police."

"Thanks. I couldn't exactly let them kill those other guys, which probably would have happened. I'd just wished the police had gotten there faster because one of them got away."

"I know, I heard." Cara looked over at me as she wiped her mouth with her napkin. "I also heard that Jackson was one of the responding officers."

I swallowed the mouthful of food I had, my stomach turning at the mention of his name. I set the muffin down on the plate in front of me and looked at my best friend. How had I forgotten how fast word traveled in small towns? I also forgot how much Ryan and Cara talked to one another. I swear they both knew that Jackson and I were having trouble in our relationship before we did. "How did you know that?"

A small smile sat on Cara's lips.

"Let me guess, Ryan?" I rolled my eyes.

"Yes, Ryan told me that a few of the guys were called

down to The Crooked Judge. Of course, it was Jackson who filled him in on the rest." She smiled. "So, what did you think?"

I looked at my best friend and shook my head. "What did I think about what?"

Cara gave me a knowing look and smiled. "Well, about Jackson. What did you think?"

I blew out a breath and shrugged, rubbing both of my temples again as the pain shot through my head at her question. "What am I supposed to think? He's still hot, I guess."

"Still hot, you guess. Bailey, any woman would have to be dead not to notice that man. Those blue eyes against that dark, tanned skin, dark, thick hair, those shoulders, abs, hands, that ass..." She winked.

"Whoa, aren't you supposed to be getting married in, like, eight weeks?"

"Yes, of course, and I'm very committed to Ryan. But come on, Bailey, you can't seriously say that you wouldn't or didn't notice him."

"I never said that. Besides, that was always the way with him, though. I can still remember the first time I ever laid eyes on him," I said, picking a piece off the muffin in front of me, getting lost in my thoughts.

"What is it?"

"It's nothing." I shrugged. Even though I was adamant that we were through, a part of me still wanted to know about him, if he was involved with someone. I wanted to know who held his heart in her hands now. "So, tell me, what do you want to plan for this wedding?"

"Oh no, don't you dare change the subject! Just ask me the question that I know is eating away at you?"

I looked at my best friend, her eyes shining with mischief. She could always read me like a book. "What question might that be?" I smiled. Two could play this game.

"Bailey, as if you don't want to know?"

"Listen, I came here to talk about someone's wedding, not about what happened last night at The Crooked Judge, nor about Jackson Walker. Now, could we please get on with things?"

Cara shrugged. "I just figured you'd want to know whether he was single because somewhere in that heart of yours, I know you're dying to ask. I also know that somewhere deep down inside, you still care about him, and don't pretend you don't."

I shook my head and looked out the window just in time to see a Sunset Cove cruiser drive down the road. I bit my bottom lip to stop the tears I could feel building in my eyes at the fact that he could very well be happily involved with someone, maybe even have kids. What bothered me the most was the fact that if he had that, then the thought of us having another chance together would be taken away instantly. I'd have lost out on him. I turned back to face the only girl who truly knew me.

"Look, he's obviously with someone. I mean, he could barely even look at me last night. He certainly didn't want to speak to me. Do you know he couldn't even ask me questions in relation to what had happened? Also, that as soon as his partner had finished, he ran out of there faster than the gang member who started the whole thing."

Cara stuck her spoon into her coffee and added another sugar packet before looking up at me. "Imagine that the man whose heart you ripped out doesn't want anything to do with you. That's shocking."

"That's a little harsh, don't you think?"

"No, I don't think it's harsh to tell the truth. You, Bailey Scott, ripped that man's heart out, tore it into little pieces, stomped on it, and left it in the dirt. Proof's in the pudding. You can ask anyone around here. They will tell you the same I am going to. That since you left, he hasn't been in one relationship, but..."

I frowned, "But what?" I questioned, waiting for her to continue.

"...but he's been with everyone."

"Everyone?" I looked at her in shock, thinking about every woman who'd wanted a piece of him when he'd been mine.

She nodded. "Sadly, yes, ever since you left. He's had

what we used to refer to as bedroom cheerleaders, but he lets no one get close to him."

I blinked to clear my vision from the tears that were now burning my eyes. The information she had just given me struck a chord, and I no longer wanted to discuss Jackson, or hear about the current sex life of my former fiancée.

"Bailey?" Cara reached across the table and placed her hand on mine. "Are you okay?"

I cleared my throat and wiped my eyes with the back of my hand. I reached into my purse and pulled out a small notebook, and began writing.

"Okay, so the wedding. We have what, about eight weeks to get this thing together?" I said, completely changing the subject, pretending everything was okay.

"Bailey?

I looked up from the notebook in front of me and met Cara's eyes. I could tell from the look on her face she knew I was upset about what she'd told me.

"I'm sorry if I upset you," she whispered.

I didn't doubt she didn't want to upset me, but hearing those words fall from her mouth had done just that. It stung knowing the truth.

"Look, you didn't upset me. I guess I'm just hurt. I have only been with one man since we split, and he's been with an entire town." I inhaled, focusing on my breath, like my therapist had taught me, and looked at Cara. "To be honest, I really don't want to talk about this anymore. So instead, let's talk about bigger, and better things, okay? Like your wedding. Now, tell me, what do you need me to do?"

She respected my wishes and reached into her purse, pulling out a purple planner, flipping it open to a page that she had scrawled some information.

"Well, I thought perhaps you could help me choose a color scheme, flowers, food selection and then arrange the seating plan. You were always good with that sort of thing."

I nodded. "Of course. Do we have a list of the wedding party and a guest list?" I said, making some notes for myself.

"We do. We are keeping it relatively small. You know, friends, family and a few work people. I think everyone has been waiting for this wedding, so we are pretty sure everyone we invite will attend. I'm just about finished with the invitations, and am hoping to get them out later today."

"Okay. That is one thing off our plates. Now, what about the wedding party?"

Cara bit her bottom lip and flipped through a few pages in her journal. Then she lifted the book up off the table toward her so I couldn't see what had been written on the page in front of her.

"We have what you would call a rough list." She said, biting her lip and looking down at the page in front of her.

"We can work with a rough list. It would help if I could I see it?" I asked, holding my hand out.

Instead of handing me the book, she dropped it off the edge of the table and down onto her lap. "No, you can't. I think we need to make a few adjustments or two, maybe three, before you see it."

I gave Cara an annoyed look. "Before I can see it? Cara, I can't make accurate plans without it. What is the problem? Why won't you let me see it? It's just a list of names."

"I just told you why. It's just a rough list."

"Cara? I don't believe it. You've probably had this list planned for nine and a half years," I said, standing up and reaching for the book, which Cara ripped away and shoved behind her back.

"You're not seeing it."

"Cara, I know you know who you want in your wedding party. Hell, you've had that list planned out when Jackson and I got engaged. I know because Ryan told him. If you don't want me to see the list, there is no way I can collaborate with anyone to get anything done. We already have a tight enough window. So that means no parties, no shower, no nothing. Now show me the book."

"Bailey, I can't."

"Why not?"

"Because you don't want to talk about Jackson."

"What? Cara, just give me the list." I said, holding my hand out.

Cara slowly placed the book in my hand, and I began reading the list. I hadn't even gotten down the list when Cara spoke.

"Because Jackson is the best man. He's your opposite in the wedding party."

I'm sure my face was filled with shock as I looked over at my friend. I should have known. It was stupid to say I wasn't expecting this, because I knew full well that he would be part of the wedding party. Ryan and he had been friends since preschool. To think he would have chosen anyone else was just foolish.

I sat there, staring down at our names listed side by side, thinking about all the things we'd be forced to do together, including walk down the aisle.

"It's okay. I'm going to have Ryan redo his side," Cara said, pulling the book back over to her.

"He's the best man?" I swallowed.

Cara nodded. "Like I said, I will have Ryan redo his list. I don't want you to be uncomfortable or to have a hard time. So, we can always just switch one of the other guys into Jackson's spot. Ryan will understand."

Even though I really didn't want to think about or see Jackson, I was here for their wedding. I needed to figure out how to work with him and put our differences aside.

There wasn't a doubt in my mind that Ryan wouldn't change it, but it wasn't fair to ask him, either.

"Look, Cara, don't," I said, reaching across the table and placing my hand on hers. "I'm here for your wedding, to stand up for two people I love dearly. I'm here to help you in whatever way I can, and I won't have Ryan redo his list. I will do my best to put aside my feelings to make your day amazing."

"Really? Are you sure?"

I nodded. "I promise. So, give me the list and I'll get started on everything."

"You're the best," Cara said, looking up at me and smiling. "I can't tell you how much this means to me."

Cara got up and came over, slid in beside me, and wrapped her arms around me. "It's great to have you back home." She whispered, hugging me tight.

# Jackson

A loud knock at the front door woke me from a deep sleep. I rolled over and listened, praying that whoever dared to knock on my door before seven in the morning would just go away.

"Get up, you ass," I heard my cousin yell from the front of the house as he banged on the door again.

"Hold on," I mumbled out loud to myself and as I kicked the covers off and grabbed the pair of jeans that lay across the end of my bed. I shoved one leg into them and then the other as I made my way down the hall. I pulled the door open, peeking out, running my hand through my hair.

"Holy shit, what the hell happened to you?" Cameron said, looking me over. I pulled the door open far enough that he could step inside.

"Nothing." I muttered, looking down at myself. Sure, I looked like an unmade bed, but hell, I was only half dressed and 5 minutes ago I'd been far off in dreamland.

"Nothing? Fuck, man, you look like shit."

"Thanks for the compliment," I grumbled, looking him over. "You don't look great yourself."

"Now I know you're lying. Was it a late-night party last night with Zoe?" He chuckled and pushed his way past me and flopped down onto the couch. He placed his feet on my coffee table, just missing the plate of the half-eaten dinner that I'd left there last night.

"Nope, worked late last night," I barked, shoving the front door closed.

"You're probably wondering why I'm here, aren't you?" Cameron chuckled, grinning up at me with his cocky-ass smile.

"Since it's not even seven in the morning, that's exactly what I'm wondering." I grumbled and flopped into my recliner, shoving the empty beer bottles that sat on the table out of the way.

Cameron shook his head in disbelief. "Well, since you've clearly forgotten, you better wake the hell up. It's our workout morning."

"Look, I'm exhausted. Maybe even still a little drunk." I shrugged, nodding to the bottles. "I'm not hitting the gym this morning, man." I leaned my head back against the chair and closed my eyes.

"I see, well, you're in luck then because I figured, instead of hitting the gym, we'd head down to the beach and go for a run. Maybe check out some chicks along the way. A last run before the snow flies."

I chuckled and ran my hands over my face. The last thing I needed to do was to go check out some chicks.

"Nah, I think the gym will serve us just fine." I ran my hand through my hair as I looked around at the mess of my living room and tried to summon some hidden ounce of energy to get ready.

"Nope, I call it. We're hitting the beach. Was it a busy night?"

"Not really."

"Then why do you look as if you've only gotten an hour's sleep?"

I looked from my cousin to the floor. I wanted to tell him why, but figured I'd just leave it alone. I didn't even know how to digest seeing Bailey again. When I'd heard she was coming back, I figured she'd bail or, if she returned, I'd be over her after all this time. I figured that the revolving turn-style my bedroom door had become screamed that. But one look into those baby blues of hers and, well, all I needed to do was look at myself in the mirror to know that I was far from over her. She'd had the same effect on me the first time I'd laid my eyes on her in high school.

"Because that's about all I've gotten." I muttered.

"Well, to make you and I feel better, go get your ass changed, and let's get going. It's a beautiful morning, and we both could use the air," Cameron said, standing up and heading into the kitchen.

"Where are you going?"

"To make a shake. I had no protein powder left." Cameron chuckled.

"You never have any left." I chuckled. "In fact, I think I went through my last container twice as fast as the one before. While you're out there, make me one too," I yelled as I made my way down to the bedroom to get changed.

The sun beat down on me and sweat poured down my back as we continued our brisk pace across the wet sand. I allowed myself to connect with the sound of the ocean, my breathing, and the pounding of my heart. Soon, the thoughts of Bailey were gone, and I finally felt like myself again. Cameron had been right. This run, this time, had been exactly what I needed.

As we approached our starting point, Cameron nodded to the main snack bar along the edge of the beach.

I nodded, and we made our way over, grabbing a cold bottle of water from their fridge. I dropped money on the counter for both bottles, nodding to the young girl behind the counter, who gave me a smile. We made our way over to a table in the shade.

"Fuck, that was a fantastic run," Cameron said, breathing hard as he twisted the cap off the bottle and drank down the cool liquid.

"It really was," I agreed and looked out over the water. The few clouds that had been in the sky had cleared, and the water was now like glass. The cooler sea air felt good against my sweaty skin.

"You all right, bro?"

I shrugged as, once again, the thoughts of Bailey invaded my mind all because I was watching a girl who looked like her set up a spot on the beach.

"I guess."

"You guess? My gut was right. You are off. What's going on with you today? Work related?"

"I don't know."

"You don't know? Are you still having those nightmares?" he questioned, resorting to the obvious of what normally bothered me.

I turned and met my cousin's eyes and nodded, half in truth. "They are always the same. I get to the end of the alley, where Connor is tucked behind a car. I can't get a good look at the guy, and then shots ring out, and down he goes. He calls for help. I look around the corner, and no one is there, so I go to him."

I close my eyes at the memory of rolling him over because he was choking, only to take pressure off the gunshot wound that ended his life. "We never should have rolled him over," I said, shaking my head. "That rule had been ingrained in us during first-aid course and every course there after: never move a victim."

"Look, you guys didn't know that the bullet had nicked the femoral artery. There would have been nothing anyone could have done, even if he had been in a hospital. The second the paramedics would have loaded him onto the stretcher, he would have bled out. It was just the pressure from his body, the way he'd been positioned, that slowed the bleeding. Even if it had been the paramedics that moved him, it would have happened. It's not your fault."

"I know, and I've paid thousands of dollars in therapy to learn that." I looked over at the girl who now sat on her beach blanket in her sweats, reading a book. "It's just the dream the other night was different."

"How so?"

I could feel my heart already racing as the memory of the dream crept slowly back into my mind, like a movie playing out. "Ryan and Grant disappeared, and I was alone in that alley with Connor. He was laying there lifeless on the pavement. I kept yelling for him to wake up and screaming for help, but no one came. Then everything around me became crystal clear and silent, and Connor sat straight up and looked right into my eyes. He asked me why I hadn't done what he'd asked. He just kept repeating those words to me. Then I woke up."

I'd talked to Cameron at length about what had happened that night. He knew everything. After all, he had been one firefighter on duty that night. He probably knew more about that night than the therapist that Grant and Ryan had finally talked me into seeing. He had been the only one I felt I could really talk to about that night. He'd seen trauma, he'd dealt with his own.

"You know, these dreams always come back around this time. I mean, we are only, what, about three months away from the anniversary of that night?" Cameron questioned.

"I know."

"So don't read into it. You know they happen every year. You need to just put it to the back of your mind and carry on. If the memories invade your mind, then you need to put your focus on something else before it gets out of control and consumes you."

"I know and I try, but sometimes I just can't. It's driving me crazy."

"I understand, but you know it's the PTSD coming forward. Maybe you need to get in with that therapist again for a couple of sessions, just to talk things through before things get out of control. I've been there. I know, and I know, how dangerous it is to allow it to take over. They can help."

My cousin was right. I went through this every year. He was also right about needing to see the therapist again. If this got out of control again, I'd go back down the same spiral.

"Jackson, I can tell you're bothered. What do you think the words in the dream meant? You think it's about Bailey, don't you?"

I looked at my cousin. "Of course it is. What else would it be about? He asked me to take care of her, Cameron, and what did I do? Instead of talking to her, instead of trying to work on things like she pleaded with me to do, I let our relationship fall apart."

"Jackson, you were not the only one responsible for what happened between the two of you. Come on now. You both suffered a tragic loss. She lost her brother, and you blamed yourself for that. It was the stress of it all that caused your relationship to crumble. You've said it yourself. She refused to get help. She refused to let things go. You were the same, certain that everything was okay when, in fact, it wasn't. You were both holding onto a lot of guilt and anger."

"I know. I just feel that, perhaps when the trouble started in our relationship, I could have fought harder. I could have tried to save us."

Cameron looked at me, concern lining his face. He sat forward, resting his forearms on his knees. "Jackson, where is all this coming from?"

"What do you mean?"

"All this, about your relationship with Bailey? Why are you suddenly beating yourself up over something that happened almost five years ago? You can't tell me this is all because of a dream you had. What gives?"

"I don't know. I just, if you had seen his face in that dream."

"Man, it was a dream. Come on."

"I know it was a dream. I just feel that the dream was trying to tell me something."

"It's telling you that you really need to forgive yourself for what happened. Call that therapist. Don't allow this to torture you the way you did for so long. I'm serious man, this shit is serious."

I looked down at the empty beach. "Perhaps you're right."

"I know I am. You know what else I am?"

"What?"

"I'm hungry. Let's go get something to eat." Cameron chuckled as he crushed the empty water bottle in his hands and stood up.

We'd devoured two grand slams at the small cafe, and then, with our stomachs full, we pulled out of the parking lot of the cafe. We drove a couple of blocks before we came to a red light. Cameron turned up a song that was playing on the radio, and I glanced around at the shoppers on the street. My heart sped up, and I had to do a double take when outside of the bridal shop on the corner I saw Cara...and Bailey.

"Ho-leeee shit," Cameron mumbled.

"What?" I asked, trying to pretend that he hadn't seen the same thing I just had. More like hoped he hadn't.

"Is that...who I think it is?" Cameron questioned; his voice lined with shock as he stared out the window. "It is. It's not a wonder why you're all fucked up. Bailey's back in Sunset Cove?"

There was no way I was going to keep the fact to myself that I too, saw her. I closed my eyes and nodded. "Yeah, you're right, that was her."

"Did you know she was back in town?"

"Yeah. I ran into her last night at The Crooked Judge." The look in her eyes flashed in my head as I thought back to last night. She'd barely said a word to me, yet that look had said so much!

"When did she get back?"

"I don't know. It was recent because Cara asked her to be her maid of honor. I wasn't sure if she had been kidding or not when she told me Bailey agreed. Honestly, I thought she'd back out when she found out I was best man, but I guess I was wrong."

As the words passed my lips, it was then I realized that she probably hadn't known that I was the best man. If she had known, I knew for a fact that she would have backed out of it.

"Well, when you ran into her, how was she?" he questioned as he sped up the car and proceeded through the light on the way back to my house.

"She looked at me the same way she did the day she walked out the door. Full of hate and blame."

Cameron grew quiet. He had been there the day she slammed the door on our relationship. We'd been doing nothing but fighting for weeks. I'd been spending more time at Cameron's than I had in my own home. When he had finally convinced me to return and work things out with her, I'd found that she had been spending the days I'd been gone packing up her stuff. The living room was full of boxes and when the realization hit that she was going to leave me, a sense of panic came over me. I didn't want to lose her.

It was three in the morning as I stood in the living room begging her to stop packing and come to bed with me, that we'd see someone together and work through everything. That was when the truth finally fell from her lips. Her words had been forever carved into my memory.

*"It's all your fault Connor died."*

The second those words had fallen from her lips, I couldn't breathe. She had just confirmed everything that I felt in my own being as being true. In that moment, I wished it had been me who died on the pavement that night. When I didn't respond to her, didn't fight back, she looked at me, tears in her eyes, and she scrambled to take those words back. It no longer mattered because everything I'd had left in me to fight for her was now gone. I couldn't be with someone who felt that way, and she could no longer hide it. She'd said those words. I stopped begging her to come to bed with me and dropped my head in defeat. I said nothing more. I just turned and headed towards our bedroom, slamming the door behind me. I'd laid in bed that night staring at the ceiling listening to her cry herself to sleep, just as I'd done the past few months. Only this time, my own tears fell down my face.

The next morning, Cameron arrived just as Bailey was carrying the last box of her stuff out to her car. We'd started fighting the second I had walked out the bedroom door. There was nothing more that we could have said. We'd spewed a lot of hateful words to one another. Once her car was packed, I watched from the front window. I watched as she hugged Cameron tightly, then she wiped tears from her cheeks, kissed him goodbye, and climbed into the car without even as much as a wave to me. When she drove away, I knew it would be the last time I saw her.

"I don't know what to say, Jackson. Perhaps if you talk to her before the wedding and get things sorted out..."

"There won't be any talking. I know full well exactly where she stands on the subject of us. That is a path, my friend, that I won't be revisiting. All I need to do is concentrate on getting through this damn wedding."

"Well, all I'm going to say is this should be interesting." Cameron said, turning onto my street.

"What is that supposed to mean?"

"Well, you'll be paired together. AT the church you'll have to walk down the aisle together, you'll be seated together for dinner, and you'll have to dance together."

I let out a breath, knowing full well that Cameron was right. "Well, I guess I'll just talk to Ryan and ask him to have Cara choose someone else." I shrugged.

"You can't do that!"

"Why not?"

"Jackson, Cara chose her. They've been friends as long as you and Ryan. Asking her to change her lineup would be wrong. How would you feel if Cara asked Ryan to change his lineup because of Bailey?"

"Fucked if I care." I shrugged.

"That's a lie and you know it. Now get your shit together and be an adult."

I opened the door and jumped out of his truck, making my way to the front door of my house. I was halfway up the walkway when I heard Cameron call my name.

"What?" I yelled back.

"What are you going to do?" He questioned.

"I'm going to get my shit together." I shrugged and opened my front door, closing it behind me.

# Bailey

Two Weeks Later

"Here is the dress," Zoe called, flying out from the storage room in a huff, carrying the dress bag over to me. "Why don't you go into this change room, slip into it, and I will have one of the girls come in here and help you."

Zoe, the owner of Sunset Cove Bridal, gave me an annoyed look as she hung the dress on the hook. I'd had to change my appointment from this afternoon to this morning because I had to work. I could hear the irritation in her voice when I called. She complained the entire time as she shuffled around her schedule to accommodate me.

"So, everything is going to be done in this small change room?" I asked, staring at the tight space. I couldn't imagine two people being in this room.

"Unfortunately, yes. I know there isn't much room, but as I told you on the phone, we have a full morning because the men of the same party are coming in to be fitted for their tuxes. Plus, I've had strict instructions from the bride that they are not to see anything in relation to any of the dresses," she said, letting out a loud huff.

"It's only a bridesmaid's dress. It's not like it's the wedding dress." I snipped back. I was tired of her attitude.

"I'm simply doing what I've been asked. I made special concessions for you to come in, otherwise I'd have told you that you'd need to find the work around. If only you'd have been able to keep your appointment, we wouldn't be having these issues."

I rolled my eyes when she turned her back away from me and unzipped the garment bag. This woman was a pill. I watched as she removed the dress from inside its garment bag when the bell above the door jingled. I looked toward the door in time to see Jackson come walking in and take a seat in the chair just inside the door.

"Be right with you," Zoe sang. "God, I hope it's not one of the men already." She said, more to herself than to me.

Jackson glanced over at me, gave me the same sexy smile he'd given me the entire time I'd known him, then grabbed his phone from his pocket and began texting someone.

"There you go, Bailey. Just slip into that, and then one

of my girls will be in to pin," she said, stepping out of the small room, pulling the curtains closed. "Whatever you do, don't..."

"Open the curtain." I know.

I locked eyes with Zoe, letting her know I was done with her attitude. She quickly averted her and walked out of the room. Irritated, I set my purse on the chair and took a minute to gather myself. Why hadn't Cara told me that Jackson would be here this morning as well? If I had known he'd be here, I'd of switched my shift at work instead. It was bad enough I was getting the attitude from Zoe.

"Jackson, you're early," I heard Zoe say in a much nicer tone than the one she'd greeted me with.

Instead of getting changed, I parted the curtain a little. I wanted to see what was going on.

"Yep, I was on my way home from work. Figured I would stop in now instead of just getting to bed, then having to get a little while later. Plus, I have to work tonight, so I'd like whatever sleep I get to be worth it."

I kept my eyes glued to Zoe, especially when I noticed how she looked at Jackson. As I watched them speaking to one another, I noticed she looked for every single opportunity she could to lay a hand on him.

"You know, it's great to see you."

When she wasn't looking Jackson glanced over his

shoulder toward my dressing room, but didn't say anything to her.

"I've given it some thought about what you said the other night. I don't want us to be over. I've really been missing you the last few nights. Think you might have a free night soon so that we can get together and talk about things?" she asked, resting her hands on his chest.

I could see the tension in Jackson's jaw as he looked down at her hands. He shook his head. "Zoe," he said, taking hold of her wrists, and removing them from his chest, "This isn't the place nor the time to discuss this. Besides, I meant what I said."

"I don't think you did. I certainly wasn't expecting you to end things with us. That wasn't the vibe I got from you the other night when you asked me to come to your place." she said, meeting his eyes and placing her hands back on his chest.

"Zoe, it's enough," Jackson said, raising his voice loud enough for me to know he was uncomfortable with her advances. "I told you, it's over between us."

I watched as her cheeks turned red and she fought to maintain her composure as she nodded. "Well, now that you've embarrassed me, I am sorry you feel that way." She mumbled as she stepped back away from him.

"Zoe, it wasn't meant to be said to embarrass you."

She nodded her head and turned away from him. "I

know, Jackson. It's okay. I'll be right back. I just want to see if one of the girls can help you out back there."

As soon as she was gone, Jackson glanced back over to the curtain I was behind. For only a moment, I was certain he'd seen me watching them, and I hoped I'd stepped back quickly enough. I prayed he hadn't seen me watching them through the crack, even though I was pretty sure he had.

I was just undoing my jeans when I heard Zoe's voice, and again I peeked between the curtains, this time to see that Jackson had now hung his jacket up. He turned back toward Zoe, giving me a glimpse of his perfect ass in a pair of tight-fitting jeans. The white T-shirt he wore hugged every muscle he had.

"All right, Jackson, we have the room set up on the other side." Zoe walked over and laced her arm through his, resting her free hand on his bicep.

An undeniable surge of jealousy fired through me. I wanted to shout out and tell her to take her hands off him, but bit my bottom lip instead, stopping myself. I had zero right to be jealous. After all, I had given him up.

"You are going to look amazing in this. Makes me wish I were going to be your date," she continued. I rolled my eyes at her comment. Could she lay it on any thicker after being told they were over? Then panic set in. Was he going to bring a date?

"Is that right?" he questioned.

"Yes. This suit will also bring out the color of your eyes."

I rolled my eyes again. Of course it would bring out his eyes, you nitwit. Sky-blue eyes against a black suit were obvious. I clenched my fists at my side and had just kicked my foot out of my jeans when the curtain was pulled open by the girl who was coming in to pin my dress. She stood there shocked that I was standing there in only my t-shirt and panties instead of the dress. Then my eyes moved to see Jackson and Zoe standing behind her.

"I was expecting you to be in your dress." She barked. "We don't have all day."

I looked at her with a scowl, and then Zoe stepped forward.

"Bailey, is everything okay? Did the dress not fit or did you need help to get into it?" Zoe questioned.

Jackson glanced over and gave me a small but very sexy smile. "Not at all," I bit out as I pulled the curtain back across without saying another word and quickly slipped into the dress.

It had been half an hour, and I stood with my jaw tight as the girl put the last few pins in the back of my dress. "All right, I think that's it," she said, running her hand over my torso. "I'll help you get out of the dress so you don't stab yourself."

A few minutes later, I pulled the curtain open in time to see Jackson come walking around the corner.

The look on his face told me he had just been put through torture, and I couldn't help but giggle to myself. I looked behind him, wondering why Zoe wasn't attached to his hip, and then I heard her. She was on the phone but watched us both from the counter as he stopped in his tracks and held his hand out in front of him, signaling for me to go first. I smiled and turned toward the counter, almost jumping as I felt his hand across my lower back.

"Hey, everything go okay?" He questioned. He was close enough to me I could feel the heat from his body, his cologne invading my senses.

I looked down at the floor, biting my bottom lip before meeting his gaze. "Hey, as well as one could expect."

"How've you been?" he asked quietly.

I shrugged, not sure what I should tell him. "I'm doing the best I can be. You?"

"Well, now that is over with, I'm much better," he said, nodding in Zoe's direction, who was now watching us intently.

I gave a tiny laugh as she shook his head in disbelief and then took a defensive tone at whatever the person on the other end of the phone was saying to her. I couldn't help but still feel a touch of jealousy, knowing that there had been something between them.

When Zoe turned around, Jackson's hand fell from

my lower back. She looked at Jackson with a longing gaze and then at me, with one of jealousy and irritation.

"So, Bailey, everything go okay?" she questioned, pulling a book out from under the counter.

I nodded. "Yes, it went fine."

"I'm glad. We will get that dress ready for you and have one last fitting before the wedding," she said, searching through her pile of invoices. "That will be one hundred and fifty for the alterations." Zoe made a few notes on my invoice. "So tell me, are you married, Bailey?"

I looked at Jackson, who shrugged as he looked at me. I squirmed uncomfortably at Zoe's question.

"No, I'm not married," I murmured, handing over my credit card. "Why?"

"Oh, I get most of my business through referrals. I figured if you knew someone or…oh never mind, don't worry, I'm sure the right one will come along soon."

I frowned. It was all I could do to keep my mouth shut as I looked over my shoulder at Jackson, who stood there with a smirk on his face. I glanced back to Zoe, who gave me a curt smile as she handed me my credit card, which I shoved back into my purse.

"See you next time." She said to me, clearly waiting for me to leave before she dealt with Jackson.

"Cara, what on earth were you thinking sending me there for a dress fitting today?"

"Hey, you were supposed to go with us. It wasn't my fault you got called into work and had to change your appointment." She looked back down at the menu in front of her and continued looking for something to order.

"You could have warned me that Jackson would be there today," I bit out as I placed a glass of water down on the bar with purpose in front of her.

Cara laughed. "I'm sorry. I guess I didn't think that through very well. Did it go okay though? I mean, was she okay to deal with?"

"Didn't think it through? Are you kidding me? You didn't think it through at all. Instead, I got to watch Zoe fall all over Jackson. You're going to look stunning in this tux. It will most definitely bring out the color of your eyes," I mimicked, grabbing Glenn and lacing my arm through his. "Wish I could be your date to the wedding," I said as I flipped my hair off my shoulder.

Cara and Glenn burst into a fit of laughter at my theatrics.

"She also loved giving me a hard time, every single chance she got. Is she like that with you, too?" I questioned.

"Yes, the last time I was in there, I had to remind her how much money I was bringing into her shop. That woman is pathetic. She is all over every man who walks in there."

"It's true," Glenn answered. "Last fall, my buddy got married. I swear that woman would have slept with all of us if given the chance."

"I could see that. Oh, you're not married, don't worry, the right one will come along." I once again mimicked while both Cara and Glenn laughed.

"I hate to end this enlightening conversation, but I've got to run to the bank. Can you handle it here?" Glenn questioned.

I looked around the empty bar and nodded. "I think I've got it under control."

Glenn nodded. "Be back shortly," he said as he walked out the front door.

I turned back to Cara. "It was probably my worst experience ever, being there with her. She was also quite demeaning."

"So, aside from mauling your man, what else did she do?" Cara asked, trying not to laugh.

"He isn't my man. However, she was downright cruel

to me. I may joke about it, but I found her to be very insulting as she stood there in front of Jackson asking me about being married."

"She was just being friendly, or maybe hoping for more business. She is new in town, and it's tough being a business owner these days. Plus, I know she gets most of her business through referral. That's how I found out about her." Cara shrugged, a funny look coming over her face.

"You found her through a referral?" I questioned. Cara and I knew the same people. There wasn't anyone in our circle who had gotten married in the past few years. "Who referred you?"

Cara looked at me and then pulled the menu back over in front of her, opening it up again.

"Are you not going to tell me?"

Again, she didn't say anything.

I looked around the bar and then back at my friend. "It was Jackson, wasn't it? They had some sort of thing together, didn't they? That's why you haven't told her to go to hell and found someone new, because you didn't want to turn your back on his referral."

"Bailey, I can explain."

"No need to don't worry about it. Just next time I go with you guys, or I will make my own appointment, opposite of Jackson."

"You know, I thought you said you were over him. The way you're acting is proving just the opposite."

"I am over him." I yelled. You could feel the tension between Cara and me as we looked at one another. I was just about to say something to her when the door to the bar opened and Ryan stepped inside.

"There's my girl," Ryan called out as he walked in the front door, followed by Jackson and Asher, each one of them nodding in our direction. Ryan came over and wrapped his arms around Cara while the other two went over to a table and took a seat.

"Hey, Bailey. Can I get three menus, please?" Ryan asked.

"Sure." I gathered the three menus and handed them to him, then watched as he headed back to the table where the others sat.

"Everything else went okay there today, though, right? The alterations, they will be done on time?" Cara asked, leaning forward. "...and please tell me he didn't see the dress, did he?" she whispered.

"No, he didn't see the dress. Honestly, other than all of that, everything went fine. I promise you, the dresses will be perfect, as will the seating arrangements and the ceremony, and I'll do my best to put the past behind. No need to turn into Bridezilla."

"I'm not. I just wanted to make sure. You do not know how much stress I am under," she whispered.

"Hey, Bailey. Good to see you," Asher said, interrupting our discussion.

I smiled. Asher and I had always gotten along. I took a minute to walk around the bar and give him a hug. As he pulled me against him, I glanced over his shoulder in time to see Jackson glance my way and then quickly avert his eyes. I caught a flash of annoyance, or jealousy in his eyes, his jaw tight. "Can we get three beers, please, Bailey," he whispered into my ear as he let me go.

"Sure thing." I quickly poured the three beers. "Ready for food yet?"

"We are still deciding. These guys can never make up their minds."

"All right, you let me know." I smiled as I placed the three beers down in front of him. He picked up the glasses and carried them over to the guys.

"So, I was wondering what you had planned for my bachelorette party?" Cara asked, grinning at me.

That was one thing I hadn't started planning. I hadn't even thought of it yet. I ran a few ideas through my mind, quickly deciding that we would have it right here.

"I just thought we could come here. You know, hang out, have some food and a couple of drinks, play some pool and dance." I said, shrugging. "Maybe retire back to your place and watch some movies. Just keep it simple."

"Well, it's a start. You will have to talk with the other

girls and figure it all out. One thing, though. I asked Ryan not to have strippers, and I want the same, okay?"

I glanced over to where the guys were sitting. Jackson sat there talking and laughing. "No strippers?" I exclaimed. "No problem." I giggled.

I began loading glasses onto the clean trays, every once in a while glancing up and looking at Jackson. God, he was so fucking attractive; I knew it would be easy to fall for him again. Too easy. I glanced at Cara and saw she was watching me with a grin on her face.

"What?"

"Why don't you just go over there and talk to him?"

"I'm not interested," I answered matter of fact.

Cara gave me a knowing look. "Bullshit, you haven't taken your eyes off that table since they walked in here. You might be able to feed that line of crap to someone else, but not to me. I know you too well."

I always had to leave it to Cara to call me out, which proved I was right. She knew me better than I knew myself.

"I wouldn't even know what to say to him if I went to talk to him. It's not like we have things to discuss."

Cara shook her head in disbelief. "Whatever you say. All I know is that you better figure things out, and soon. I can't have you two dripping with all this tension during the wedding."

"There is no tension." I bit back. Just as the words

rolled off my tongue, Asher caught my attention and my eyes instantly landed on Jacksons. I could feel my face heat as Cara watched me. I grabbed my notepad and made my way around the bar. "There won't be any tension, I promise."

"Whatever you say." She called after me as I walked away.

# Jackson

I had been looking forward to this night since I'd agreed to be part of the wedding party. At first, I'd figured we'd hit a strip joint, have some food and beer, and perhaps play a few games of pool. That bubble burst when Ryan came to me and told me Cara asked him not to have strippers at his own bachelor party. I was taken aback. Who the hell made agreements like that? So instead of being a man and standing up to Cara, here we all sat in Ryan's living room playing games on the PlayStation.

Tonight was supposed to be about stress relief. Only, I ended up getting roped into picking up the girls from the bachelorette party and getting them home safely if they needed a ride, which meant I had to stay sober. Ryan owed me huge; I thought as I looked around the kitchen.

The table was littered with pizza boxes, crumpled napkins, and empty beer and pop cans we scattered everywhere.

A loud roar of laughter came from the living room as the guys completed another round of some racing game they'd been playing. Ryan stood in the corner of the kitchen loading up a plate of cold wings while I started collecting some of the empty cans.

"Is this really all you wanted to do tonight?" I questioned.

Ryan chuckled. "Listen, I know you were hoping for a little tits and ass, but I'm not putting myself into any type of situation that might mess up this wedding. Cara means the world to me."

"I never said you had to do anything to mess it up, but really, what is a bachelor party without some tits?"

Ryan laughed at my comment. "Look, I'd die without Cara, and to be honest, with you, when she asked me not to have strippers, what could I say? So, I am just respecting her wishes."

"Always Mr. Respectful, huh? I call it pussy whipped." I coughed.

"Call it what you want. However, you are the one who isn't drinking tonight because a certain someone is out with the girls and may need a ride home. You're also standing there cleaning up the kitchen because you know Cara will flip a bird if she sees this place like this. Who's the pussy whipped one now?"

I'd been burned by my best friend. I could play it up all I wanted. I could say that I was just doing my duty as the best man but when Cara asked that I stay sober to make sure the girls got home safely, but I already knew the truth. The girls who were out with them tonight barely drank. Cara had already stated that she would probably remain sober the entire night since she'd had a severe headache most of the day. Truthfully, I was worried that Bailey may not. She'd always been a bit of a party animal, and I was sure being back here wasn't the easiest thing for her to be dealing with.

"Not pussy whipped at all, just doing my job as the best man." I replied as I cracked open another can of soda and drank down the cold liquid. I grabbed a slice of pizza from the box and had taken a bite when Asher walked into the kitchen.

"You guys need to get in there. I'm getting my ass handed to me in this game," he said, grabbing wings and a slice of pizza just as the phone rang.

"Come on, let's go see if I can't beat the lap you're on just like I used to do when you were just a pain in the ass kid." I said, grabbing Asher by the back of the neck and guiding him to the living room.

"Hey, Jackson," Ryan called just as I was about to sit down. I walked over to where my friend stood, clenching the phone in his hand. "Can you head down to The Crooked Judge? Cara says that she needs some help."

I frowned. "What's going on?"

"She won't say. She just said she needs your help."

I glanced at Asher and shrugged. "You're on your own." I smirked, then dug my hand into my pocket and pulled my keys out. "Tell her I'm on my way," I said, shoving the rest of my pizza into my mouth.

Just as the door slammed behind me, both Ryan and Asher yelled, "Go get her, show her what she's missed out on." Laughter erupted from inside as I rolled my eyes and gave them both the finger as I climbed into my truck.

It took about twenty minutes before I walked into The Crooked Judge. The place was packed, and it took me a minute to spot Cara and one of the other girls over by the pool tables. I waved, then made my way through the crowd to them.

"Hey, Jackson," Cara greeted me, a worried look on her face.

"Where is everyone?" I questioned, looking into the sea of patrons that filled the bar.

"Most of the girls left around eleven. We were going to join them and head to Sierra's place for a movie, but Bailey wouldn't come with us. I wasn't leaving her here alone," she said, nodding toward the bar. I turned around and saw Bailey sitting on a barstool. She was milking a beverage while Marcus, the only bartender I couldn't stand in this entire establishment, stood there in front of her. He leaned down on the bar, running his finger down her cheek as she flirted back.

"How long has this been going on?" I asked, some form of jealous rage coming over me as I kept my eyes glued to Marcus.

"It's been going on a while. He's been hitting on her all night. The more she drank, the more attention he showed her. Apparently, he's taking a real liking to her, and she told me he started getting handsy during their shared shifts here. She was complaining to me the other day about him. Regardless, he's been buzzing around us all night. An hour ago, he convinced her to go up to the bar. That's when he started pouring her shots." Cara said, looking at me with a worried expression.

I knew Bailey had a low tolerance for alcohol and could only imagine what she would be like if she'd been downing shots. "How many do you think she's had?" I questioned, watching them more carefully now.

"We lost count, but once she started drinking those, the less she interacted with us, right to where she didn't want to leave no matter what I said. I don't trust this guy, Jackson, and we didn't want to leave her alone, but Sierra's waiting for us to arrive at her place."

I blew out an irritated breath. "Look, you go. I'll make sure she gets home, okay?"

"You sure? I mean, I will stay if you want."

I glanced at Cara and gave her a knowing look.

"Please, I think I know how to handle her. You also know I would let nothing happen to her. Go, have fun, okay?" I said, pressing a kiss to her cheek. "I'm glad you called."

Cara smiled, leaned in, and kissed my cheek, then threw her arms around me. "You always were a good guy, Jackson. Look after my girl." She winked, then grabbed her purse and headed to the door.

I waited until the girls were gone. That gave me time to watch and see exactly what was going on. Marcus set another drink down, along with another shot, down on the bar in front of Bailey. I frowned and looked at a very drunk Bailey. From the looks of it, she really didn't need anything else to drink as she swayed on the stool. The second Marcus turned and walked away to serve another customer, I walked over and leaned against the bar beside Bailey, placing my arm on the back of her chair.

"Hey."

She looked up at me, squinting until I came into focus. "What—where—what are you doing here?"

"I think it's time we get home. Looks like the party is over here." I said, leaning into her.

She turned and looked up at me, a low chuckle escaping her lips. "No thanks, I'm good," she said, raising the shot in the air and downing it.

"Aren't you tired?" I questioned.

She picked up the shot and grimaced as she swallowed

the clear liquid, then smiled at me and placed the shot glass down on the bar top. "Nope."

"I beg to differ. I think it's time for you to get home and get into bed. Come on, let's go." I gripped her arm, which she ripped away from my grasp. She lost her balance and almost fell from the chair. I grabbed hold of her, securing her against me before she fell over, holding her until she got her bearings.

"You okay?" I asked, meeting her eyes.

"Why are you always so good to me?" she grumbled, resting her head on my chest, closing her eyes for a split second.

"What can I get for you?" Marcus asked, eyeing me as Bailey pulled away the second she heard his voice. He gave me a glaring look and then looked at Bailey and signaled for her to drink up.

"I'll have water."

He quickly got me a glass of cold water, which I set down in front of Bailey, removing the other untouched drink from her reach.

"Hey, give me that." Bailey cried, reaching for the glass.

"No. I think you should drink this instead. It's better for you."

"But I don't want it. I want that one," she said, pointing to the glass I had moved away from her.

"I'm sure you do, but I think you've had enough."

Bailey looked over at Marcus and waved her hand. He looked me directly in the eyes as he brought over another shot and set it down in front of her. Before I could stop her, she picked it up and pounded it back, making a face.

"Bailey, come on, let's go. I'm going to take you home."

"I'm fine, Jackson," she slurred.

"Listen, man, she's fine. I'll take her home," Marcus gritted.

"Oh, I'm sure you would. Just like you'd probably take a little something else in the duration." I said, glaring at him. "What does she owe?" I questioned.

"Two hundred and twenty," Marcus said, smirking. "What can I say? Your girl likes to drink."

I completely ignored his comment and pulled my credit card from my wallet, handing it to him. It was a small price to pay knowing I was saving her from a man who clearly only wanted one thing, and the fact that he had gotten her drunk to attain it made me sick. I had a good mind to charge him. If I could have proved it, I would have.

"Come on, Bailey,"

Bailey turned her watery, bloodshot eyes on me and shoved at my chest. "He's taking me home," she said, nodding toward Marcus.

I looked over at Marcus, who could barely keep his eyes off her. The look he gave was making me incredibly uncomfortable. Marcus threw my credit card down on the counter. I looked at Bailey, who now had her head down on the bar. I knew it was going to be only a matter of minutes before she passed out. In all the years I'd been with her, I'd never seen her this drunk.

"Come on, beautiful, let's get you home," I said in her ear.

This time, she didn't fight me. Once my arm was wrapped around her, she slowly and unsteadily stood up, leaning against me. I stopped to get a better grip on her and that was when she looked up at me, squinting.

"We should dance. Remember how we used to dance? You'd hold me like you'd never let me go," she mumbled. Just then, one of her favorite songs came over the speakers. "Hold me like that again, Jackson," she whispered as she wrapped her arms around my neck, pressing her body into me. "Whisper the words in my ear, the way you used to."

I readjusted my arm around her to make sure she wouldn't fall and guided her to the door. I pulled her against me, holding her with one arm while waiting for a group of people to exit the bar.

"You smell so good. Just how I remembered," she muttered, burying her face into the crook of my neck, the soft puff of breath sending shivers through my body.

I nodded to the bouncer, who held the door open for me. I led her outside, the cold air hitting us both as we stepped out onto the sidewalk. I took my time, carefully leading her to my car, and opened the passenger door. Once I got her seated and her belt done up, I closed the door and made my way around to the driver's side.

"Where are you staying? With your mom?" I questioned as I turned the engine. When she didn't respond, I glanced over at the passenger's seat to see Bailey had already passed out, her head resting against the headrest. I tapped the steering wheel with my right hand and thought for a moment. There was no way I could show up at her mom's house with Bailey in this condition. Her mother worried enough about her. I didn't want to give her cause to worry more. I also couldn't take her back to Ryan and Cara's. I wasn't sure if she had a place of her own. There was only one thing I could do, and I was sure my decision would open up a can of regret as I pulled away from the curb, heading toward my place.

It took me a bit, but I finally got her inside the house. I turned on the small table lamp at the end of the couch and placed her on the couch. I tucked a pillow under her head and was just going to leave her there when she started to dry heave. I quickly rushed to the kitchen, grabbed a bowl, and returned just in time to watch as she got sick all over herself.

"Fantastic," I muttered, setting the clean bowl on the table. "Cara owes me big time." I mumbled as I ran down the hall and grabbed one of my T-shirts, returning to the living room. I carefully slipped her soiled shirt off over her head and slipped my T-shirt on in its place, then I gently pulled her out of her jeans. I looked down at her as she rolled onto her side and curled her bare legs up to her. Pulling the blanket off the back of the couch, I covered her and placed the bowl on the floor beside the couch.

I balled her clothes up and threw them into the washer, starting the load. When I returned to the living room, I watched her for a moment. Then went to the kitchen, poured a glass of water, and dropped two headache tablets in the palm of my hand. I returned to the living room, leaving the pills and water on the table in front of her. There was no doubt in my mind she would need them when she woke up. I sat down and watched her for a bit, making sure she wasn't going to be sick again. When I was certain she was going to be fine, I pulled the covers up over her shoulder and shut the light off.

I stood watching her bathed in the light from the streetlight. I'd forgotten how beautiful she was. I felt more at ease knowing that she was here, safe from that creep. After everything that had happened, I doubted I would get any sleep tonight, but I walked down the hall to the bedroom, anyway. Once in my bedroom, I slipped out of my jeans, pulled my shirt off over my head, and crawled into bed.

# Bailey

I rolled over and could already feel my stomach threatening to empty its contents. I felt like I was already spinning, and it only worsened when I opened my eyes. The bright light from the window practically blinded me, and I buried my head back into the pillow. The clang of metal aggravated my already aching head as I rubbed at my dry eyes and lifted my head, pain running through my temples.

I looked around the room and then down at the unfamiliar, oversized T-shirt I was wearing. I looked at the table where there was a glass of water and, beside that, two headache tablets. I reached for them, popping them into my mouth and drinking down the warm water.

There was another loud bang from the other room, and I sat up and kicked the covers off me to find I was missing my pants. I took a deep breath, recognizing the old worn material of the La-Z-Boy chair that was across from me. I had purchased that chair for Jackson when we had moved in together. What the hell was I doing at Jackson's? I stood up, waited for the room to stop spinning, and glanced around the room one more time before making my way into the kitchen.

Jackson stood at the counter, shirtless, the muscles of his back rippling as he whipped whatever he had in the bowl. I leaned against the door frame and took in the view. He continued whipping the contents of the bowl. The clanging of the metal against metal drilled into my head. "Can you please just stop that?" I bit out, rubbing my temples as pain shot through them again.

He turned abruptly, as if I had caught him doing something he shouldn't have been. "Sleep well?" he asked, a small smile creeping onto his lips for a minute before he went back to whipping the contents of the bowl.

"What am I doing here?" I demanded.

Jackson let out a throaty laugh. "Better here than where you could have ended up."

"What's that supposed to mean?" I crossed my arms across my chest, getting my defenses up. "Where are my clothes?" I questioned, trying to piece together any memory of what had happened last night.

"Your clothes are in the dryer, right over there. You got

sick all over yourself," he muttered, then turned and placed two glasses of juice down on the table.

I looked from him to the dryer. "You... you undressed me?" I questioned.

"You didn't leave me much choice. It was that or I let you sleep in your own filth all night, and since you were sleeping on my couch, I decided to be nice. Now sit down," he said, nodding to the chair.

I glanced at the couch where I'd woken up and then did as I was told. I was too tired, and my head hurt too much to fight back. I was not only was embarrassed about last night, but suddenly felt dizzy and was afraid I was going to be sick.

"My God, I'm so humiliated," I said as I placed my face in the palms of my hands.

Jackson dropped batter into the hot pan and waited for a couple of seconds before flipping the pancakes in the pan. Then he placed a few strips of bacon down on the griddle, the aroma filling the air.

"You know, you really shouldn't get that drunk. If you think you are humiliated now, you'd have been much more humiliated if I hadn't of stopped by The Crooked Judge on my way home, that much I can promise you."

"I was with Cara and the girls, Jackson. I was safe."

"Yep, you're right, you were. Until they wanted to leave, and you wanted to stay with Marcus."

"Marcus?"

"Yeah, as in Marcus, your co-worker."

I could already see where this conversation was headed. We'd be right back into another argument. I didn't even remember talking to Marcus, so I wasn't sure if Jackson was telling me the truth or making it up. "Marcus? What does Marcus have to do with this?"

"He was serving up a storm. He planned on taking you home last night. That was until I showed up. He would have had his hands all over you if given the chance. Which I am sure he would have gotten, judging from the state you were in. God, it fucking pisses me off to know end thinking about what might have happened to you."

I frowned, looking at how tense the muscles in his forearm were from holding the flipper. "You don't own me, Jackson." I rubbed the sleep out of my eyes, my head still pounding.

"No, you're right, I don't. However, I'm still not going to let that dog get his hands on you and take advantage of you."

"Please. I work with him. What do you think he was going to do?"

"Yes, you work with him, and according to Cara, you were also complaining about him coming on to you and being handsy on shift one night."

"Cara! What does Cara have to do with this? Oh wait, you didn't stop by on your way home, did you? Cara called you?"

I watched as Jackson's shoulders moved in a silent laugh. "Bailey, you always were the innocent one. Yes, Cara called me because she was concerned about you."

"Jesus." I whispered under my breath as I ran my fingers through my hair. "I was perfectly capable of taking care of myself, Jackson. She didn't need to call you."

Jackson spun around and met my eyes. I could see the anger in them. "Really? You think so?"

"I know so."

"Right. You were practically hanging off of me when I walked you from the bar to the car and I carried you in here."

I shook my head. He had to be wrong. "No, that's not true." I didn't want to hear anymore about what had happened last night, but I had a feeling he was going to tell me anyway.

"Let's see. We were standing outside the door when you finally came to. The first thing you did was run your hand over my crotch and tug at my belt. I almost forgot how turned on you'd get once you had a few." He chuckled.

"Oh my god." I gasped and then grew quiet. Jackson was right, I was a mess. I was a mess for many reasons, him being one of them. The scene in the bridal shop I'd witnessed a couple of weeks ago, as that woman fawned all over him, had struck some underlying chord within me.

"Look. Bailey, I was only kidding about the crotch

grab. I just wanted you to realize that you weren't in control last night. You also need to know that I didn't bring you back here for any other reason than to make sure you had a safe place to sleep. I certainly don't want to argue with you." Jackson mumbled as he placed the plate of fresh steaming pancakes and two slices of bacon down in front of me, then handed me the syrup. "Truce."

I looked up into those blue eyes of his and felt an overwhelming sense of protection coming from him. I couldn't help myself as a tear slipped from my eye. I reached for the syrup. "Thank you." I sniffled.

He winked at me. "You're welcome." He pulled the chair out across from me and sat down, quickly taking a bite of bacon before digging his fork into the pile of fluffy pancakes.

"Look, we can't fight. We can't ruin Ryan and Cara's wedding because of our past. So we need to find a way to get along."

"I agree. It wouldn't be right. So, what do you propose?" He questioned.

I thought for a minute. "I guess we do our best to get along. Then, after the ceremony, toast, dinner, cake, and the last dance of the evening, our truce is over. We can then go on our own way."

A cocky smile fell onto Jackson's lips, one I'd come to know well. "So, I guess what you are telling me is that I only have a few short weeks to win you over before the end of that night, huh?"

I almost choked at his suggestion. "I doubt Zoe would approve of your plan," I bit out.

Jackson looked at me, a serious expression on his face. "Zoe isn't in the picture now, is she?"

"I don't know, you tell me?"

"No, she isn't, for many reasons," he said, looking down at his plate. "Honestly, I wouldn't walk a single step for her, but to have another chance with you? Well, I'd do just about anything."

I didn't know how to react to that. I studied his eyes and could see the seriousness in them. "Yeah, well, good luck with that."

"What is that supposed to mean?"

"You aren't that smooth."

A laugh ripped from Jackson's throat, and he set his blue eyes on me. Silence fell between us. His blue eyes danced, and if I allowed myself, I knew it would be only a matter of minutes before I was lost in them, because that would be all it took. His eyes, looking at me, the way they used to.

"I know for a fact at one point you would have disagreed with yourself. However, we aren't going to argue because we can't ruin Cara and Ryan's wedding," he said, smiling smugly at me again.

He was so damn cute, but I hid my smile and instead

nodded in agreement. There was no way I was giving into him that easily. The dryer buzzed and interrupted the look between us. Jackson jumped up and left the room, leaving me to sit there alone. I took a deep breath. No matter how confused I may have been with everything or how much I held on to the past, I knew one thing. That this man was going to be the death of me.

He came back into the kitchen; in his hand he held my clothes. I used to love the feel of his hands on me and wondered if they still felt the same—tender but strong.

"What is it?" he asked as he placed my dry clothes on the back of the empty chair beside me.

I shook my head and picked up my fork, digging into the stack of pancakes. "Nothing."

"Bailey? What is it?"

"I was just thinking my mom must be worried sick about me," I answered, hoping I was hiding what was really on my mind.

"Is that where you're staying? With your mom?"

I nodded, taking another mouthful of food. "I told her I would be home last night. God, she is probably worried sick."

"Well, I figured you might stay there, but there was no way I was going to show up on your mom's doorstep with you in that shape. So, how about I take you home after we finish breakfast?"

I nodded. "Thanks."

"No worries. You can call her," he said, pointing to the phone.

I shook my head. "No, it's okay. The last thing I need is my mom to see your number on her call display."

"Better mine than Marcus's?" Jackson said, letting out a laugh.

I could see my Mom on her hands in knees in the front garden as Jackson pulled into the driveway of the small bungalow. She glanced over her shoulder when she heard the car, at first a look of concern on her face and then a small smile. I sat there, almost frozen, as she stood up, dusted off the knees of her jeans, and walked over to the car.

"A word of warning," I said, turning to look at him. "She's been asking about you."

"That's okay." He said, putting his truck into park.

"It's really not," I murmured as Mom approached the car just as Jackson hit the button for the window and rolled it down.

"Good morning." He grinned.

"Morning, Jackson. I see you brought our princess home safe and sound. Bailey, I was so worried when I woke up and you weren't here. Why didn't you call me?"

"Sorry about that." I swallowed hard, hoping she didn't ask any more questions, or worse, that Jackson told her how he had found me.

"It's okay. I know you were in excellent hands now." She said, glancing at Jackson.

"How are you doing, Mrs. Scott?"

"Oh, Jackson, don't be ridiculous. I think we are long past the Mrs. Scott nonsense."

"You are right. How are you doing, Donna?" he corrected.

Mom stood there laughing as she pulled off one of her gardening gloves to push a strand of hair back off her face. "I'm fine. Always tending to the gardens."

"They are looking great." He smiled. "Think you might win that award this year?"

"Thanks. I certainly hope so. So, did you two have a good time last night?" she asked, leaning down on the edge of the car.

Jackson glanced over at me, waiting for me to answer. I cleared my throat. "Yep, great time. Jackson, thanks for the drive home. Seriously, though, I could have taken an Uber from Cara's."

Mom looked from me to Jackson and back to me, and the uncomfortable feeling settled around me. I hated lying to her.

"You could have, but then I wouldn't know where to find you, now would I?" He reached out and tweaked my chin.

Mom let out a little giggle. "I'll give you two some privacy and let you say goodbye," she said, and made her way back over to the flowers she'd been working on.

I turned and met his eyes, which were full of laughter, and shook my head. The last thing I needed was my mother to think we were getting back together. I pushed the car door open and climbed out and was about to close the door when he yelled out loud enough for my mother to hear, "I'll call you later. Maybe we can see that movie."

I turned around. He sat there with that sexy smile on his face while I glared at him. "Don't do this, Jackson.," I said through clenched teeth, keeping my voice low enough that my mother couldn't hear. He sat there grinning at me as I closed the door and walked away from the car.

"I'll see you soon!" he yelled as he waved and backed out of the driveway.

I sighed and made my way up to where my mom was sitting digging out weeds.

"Well, that was a pleasant surprise. Did you guys have a good time last night?"

"It was okay."

"Just okay?" She questioned, looking at me. "Bailey, I'm glad to see you are working things out between the two of you?" Mom stood up from where she'd been sitting and brushed off her pants.

"We aren't getting back together, Mom. He was there at Cara and Ryan's this morning, and he did me a favor and brought me home," I said, heading up the front stairs of the house.

"But you took your car to Cara's," Mom said, stopping me in my tracks. "I saw it there when I went out to the garden center this morning."

I bit my bottom lip and frantically searched my mind for an excuse. "It wasn't my car, Mom. Sierra has the same car I do. I left mine downtown last night. Now, I need to go shower."

# Jackson

It's been two weeks since Bailey spent the night on the very couch I was now relaxing on. We had been spending a lot of time together during those couple of weeks working on the plans for Cara and Ryan's wedding. We'd spent nights sending texts back and forth, about the events for the actual wedding that Cara and Ryan both didn't want to take on. However, occasionally, the conversations would become fun and flirty. It was something that I could only dream about.

Now that the wedding was drawing near, I was hearing from her less and less, yet she barely left my mind. We'd both been spending time with Cara and Ryan separately and not so much with each other. She claimed that everything we could do together had been done. So you can imagine how surprised I was when my phone rang and I saw her name on the screen.

"Hello," I answered, turning the TV down.

"Hey, what are you doing?" she asked. I could hear loud music in the background and guessed she was probably at work.

"Trying to find something on TV. You?"

She cleared her throat. "I was wondering if you felt like getting out of the house?"

Sitting forward, I muted the television. I could tell from the tone in her voice that something was up. I cleared my throat and thought twice about asking her the question I wanted to know the answer to for fear she thought I was trying to protect her. "Are you all right? What's going on?"

"It's just quiet at work tonight. Just wanted some company." She said, a slight quiver in her voice.

I flipped the TV off, threw my T-shirt over my head, and grabbed my keys. I had a feeling deep in my gut that something wasn't right. "On my way."

Twenty minutes later, I walked through the door of The Crooked Judge. I expected the place to be empty but was shocked to find that the place was almost full. Judging from the fact that Bailey had commented on how quiet it was, now I knew something was wrong. She was behind the bar preparing an order, so I just straddled a stool at the end of the bar where she was working away and waited for her to turn around.

She'd placed the last pint of beer on a tray and passed it to one server, and then her eyes met mine. A soft smile came to her lips as she approached me.

"Thought you said the place was dead?" I said, looking over my shoulder at the crowd, then back at her. "Or did you just miss me?" I winked, then chuckled.

She was about to say something, but stopped, an uncomfortable look coming over her face. I turned and looked over my shoulder in the direction she was looking and spotted Marcus walking out from the back room carrying a case of beer. She didn't need to say any more. I could tell from the look on his face the second he made eye contact with me exactly what had been going on and why Bailey had called.

"What can I get for you?" she asked as Marcus glared at me, slamming the case of bottles down on the back counter.

"I'll have a soda and a burger if the kitchen is still open." I said, winking at her. She needed to know I would not leave her here alone with him.

He walked over and dropped a dish of peanuts in front of me, glaring my way.

By the time Bailey had placed my order and filled a glass, Marcus had returned to the back room. She brought it over and set it down in front of me, giving me a very uncomfortable look.

"He giving you trouble again?"

She looked at me and nodded. "He has barely kept his hands to himself, despite being told a hundred times. I've put in a complaint, and I'm sure Glenn spoke to him. He was angry yesterday. Then today, well, I fear my complaint only made it worse," she whispered, for fear he may hear, which would be impossible over the loud music.

"You have a ride home?" I asked, glancing down at my watch.

"No, I loaned Mom my car tonight. Hers is in the shop. She had things to do. So she dropped me off. I was just going to take a cab."

I shook my head. "No need. I'll wait until you are done with your shift."

"Jackson, no, that is two in the morning," she said, shaking her head.

"Bailey, do I need to remind you I stay up all night more than half my works shifts? It's not a big deal. I'm not leaving you alone here with him."

She looked at me and shook her head. "No, you don't need to remind me. I just don't want him to get angry."

"Bailey, I dare him to get angry. I'd rather him take it out on me than on you, and that is why I'm not leaving. I don't trust him."

"Jackson, please, don't make me regret calling you

here." She said, biting her bottom lip. She didn't need to tell me she was afraid. I could see it in her eyes.

She was afraid of him, and for that reason alone, she could refuse all she wanted. I refused to hear it, so waiting was exactly what I did. I sat at the end of that bar until two in the morning, waiting and watching for him to make a move. When closing time hit, the music went off, and I watched as Marcus escorted patrons out the front door. Once the bar was empty, he turned to me.

"Hey, buddy, it's time to get going." He said, shooting his thumb toward the door.

"Yep, and as soon as Bailey is ready, we will be on our way." I grinned.

Marcus furrowed his brow and looked me over. "You can wait outside for her. Can't have people inside when we are closing. Gotta count the money. Owner's rules," he said, approaching me and placing his hand on my shoulder.

I looked down at his hand and back up at him. "Trust me, I won't be a bother," I said, throwing another handful of nuts into my mouth and looking at Bailey as she stood by watching, the look of fear settling on her face.

Marcus grabbed my arm and tried to remove me from my seat. I shoved him in the chest and growled. "Get your hands off of me."

"Buddy, I'm not going to ask you again. I said it's time

to go," he said, this time smartening up and not touching me.

Standing up and extending to my full height, I towered over him at six feet. I looked down into his face. "And I said I wouldn't be a bother," I responded, reaching behind me and pulling out my badge, flipping it open for him to see. I didn't enjoy flipping that on anyone, especially when I was off duty, but this guy was making me angry.

He released his hold on me immediately and straightened the wrinkles he had caused in my shirt. "I'm sorry. We will get this place closed shortly." He began walking toward the bar and then stopped. "Bailey, on second thought, why don't you head home early? I'll take care of everything," He said, running around behind the bar, taking over for her at the dishwashing station.

"We aren't supposed to close alone."

"It's fine. Go. I won't say anything to the owner."

I nodded to Bailey, who looked over at me with concern in her eyes. I knew she was afraid Glenn would give her shit in the morning, and if it came to it, I'd speak to him. She finally grabbed her purse and light jacket, and together we headed out the door and over to my car.

"Jackson, really, was that necessary?" she asked once we were in the car.

"Look, the guy was giving you the creeps, or you wouldn't have called me."

"But I'm going to get into trouble."

"No, you aren't. You let me know if Glenn has words with you on this. If he does, I'll talk to him. They may be interested in knowing what Ben's serving protocols are." I said, referring to the number of drinks I'd witnessed him giving Bailey when she was clearly intoxicated. "Do up your belt."

She did as I asked without hesitation, and I pulled away from the curb, heading towards her mom's house.

The rest of the week had flown by, and by Friday night, the entire wedding party was seated at a long table in one of the event rooms of the hotel for the rehearsal dinner. I sat there, lost in my own thoughts and memories, thinking about Bailey and I. We had only just begun planning our wedding when we'd broken up. We'd actually planned on having our wedding reception in this very hotel and I wondered what would have happened had it of happened. I was deep in thought when I heard my name and realized everyone at the table was looking at me, waiting for a response to a question I hadn't heard.

"All I can say is that I hope you don't do this

tomorrow when I ask you to pass the rings," Ryan said, laughing.

Laughter erupted, and I glanced across the table at Bailey, a soft smile on her lips. She met my eyes for just a second before Cara stood and held her glass for a toast. Afterward, she broke out into a few announcements about the rest of the evening and tomorrow.

Fifteen minutes later, everyone began clearing the room, some going back to their rooms, others heading down to either the lounge or spa.

"Are you coming, Bailey?" Cara questioned, glancing at me, noticing I was watching them.

"Maybe in a bit," Bailey said, smiling in her direction.

"All right, I will hold you a spot in case you want to join, okay?"

I watched as Bailey nodded, then reached into her purse and pulled out a card. I frowned. She seemed happy, but I knew the fake smile was just that. Deep down inside, something was on her mind. I waited until the room had cleared and stretched. Bailey glanced up from whatever it was she was writing. "Aren't you going with the guys?" she asked.

"I told them I'd meet up with them soon. I need to let this food digest before I get into the drinks."

"I see."

"What about you? What are you going to do now?" I asked, walking around to her side of the table and leaning down beside her, a waft of her vanilla-scented shampoo hitting my nose.

She glanced at me and smiled. "A few of the girls are going to have a spa treatment. They asked me if I wanted to join, but I think I'm just going to take a walk in the park. I need to get some air."

Our eyes locked, and she looked at me as if she wanted to say something. I waited, but she said nothing, just sat there looking into my eyes.

"You feeling okay?" I questioned. Her cheeks were flushed, and her eyes looked darker than normal.

She nodded and smiled again, only this time the smile didn't reach her eyes. There was something bothering her. I knew that look way too well. "I'm okay. Just tired, I guess. I haven't been sleeping very well, and it has been a long day," she mumbled, popping the envelope back into her purse before turning to look at me. "Good night. Hope you have fun with the guys tonight. I will see you tomorrow."

There were so many things I wanted to say to her. Mostly, I wanted to lean in and give her a kiss. Instead, she surprised me by putting her hand on my chest, leaning in and placing a gentle kiss on my cheek before she stood up. She gathered her things, and I watched as she took her time walking out of the room. I heard a familiar laugh and looked around. Ryan stood off in the corner speaking with one of the hotel employees.

In a matter of minutes, he was by my side. "Sorry, just had to take care of a last-minute dietary restriction. You ready for some drinks or what?" he said, gripping my shoulders. "I sure as hell am. I'm hoping it takes my mind off what I'm about to do tomorrow." He chuckled.

"In a few. I'm just going to take a breather for a half hour, maybe run up to my room, get changed. I'll meet you there?"

"Sure, but you better be ready to drink your face off for my last night of being single. I can't experience this night without my best friend at my side."

"You know me. I'm always up for drinking my face off." I laughed.

"Awesome! Okay, see you soon," Ryan called as he made his way toward the bar.

I watched until Ryan disappeared out of sight. I had no intention of going back to my room. Instead, I took off out the front door of the hotel and wandered across the street into the park. I'd spent the entire evening sitting across from Bailey. I'd also spent most of that time wondering where we might have been if we had chosen a different path. We'd have been married by now. We might have even had a couple of kids. Instead, I was sitting across from her at our best friends' wedding like we were strangers.

I walked through the park, finally taking a seat on a bench. A half hour had passed when I finally saw her walking toward me. She walked slowly, her head down as if she were deep in thought. My heart rate sped up as she came toward me. God, she was gorgeous. I just wanted to stare at her, without her knowing for a little while longer, but she glanced up in time to meet my eyes.

Surprise lined her face. "What are you doing out here?" she questioned as she approached. "I figured you'd be knee deep in the scotch about now." She let out the cutest giggle and glanced at her watch.

God, that giggle. The same one that I fell in love with so long ago had returned for the first time since she had. It was so good to hear it again. I shook my head. "I just needed to let all that food settle. I told Ryan I'd be along after. Why don't you take a seat?" I said, patting the bench beside me.

She walked over and sat down beside me, tucking her purse between us. She leaned back and looked up into the trees, then closed her eyes and took a deep breath. I couldn't help but study her face. How I wished she would allow me to get close to her again.

We both sat there in silence, each looking off in the distance, unsure of what to say to one another.

"Are you okay?" she questioned, concern lining her voice. It was only a second before I felt her hand on the back of my head as she ran her fingers through my hair. I closed my eyes and allowed myself to enjoy the feeling of her touch for the first time in years.

"I am. Just a lot of memories surfacing," I whispered. "What about you? Enjoy tonight?"

"Yeah, it was okay, I guess." She avoided my eyes this time.

I sat back on the bench and stretched my arm across the back of it. It surprised me when she moved closer, leaned into me, and rested her head on my shoulder. At first, I didn't know what to do, but then I wrapped my arm around her and pulled her closer to me.

"You know, I was thinking during dinner that I wouldn't have gone with the chicken dish at our wedding."

"Oh?"

"And what about that dessert? The one with the custard."

"It was so gross," we both said in unison.

Like music to my ears, Bailey giggled again. "What would you have gone with?" she questioned.

"I don't know, probably steak, and some sort of cherry dessert, like that cheesecake your mom makes. I've been craving it for a while now."

"Yes, god I haven't had that in ages." She whispered, then grew quiet. She interlaced her fingers with mine, snuggling into me a little closer. I closed my eyes and rested my head against hers, allowing the scent of her shampoo to surround me.

We both sat there, quiet, just holding one another for

a while, and then she cleared her throat. "Whatever happened to us?" she whispered. "Why did we allow all of what happened to... split us apart?"

I sat there, running my thumb over the back of her hand, holding her against me. I didn't have an answer. I didn't even know if she wanted an answer. Truthfully, I was afraid to even move because I didn't want to stop her from continuing with this conversation, especially if she had more to say.

"You know, Jackson, I've thought a lot about that over the last few years, more so over the last few weeks. From the second I first saw you again, I realized how much I've missed you."

I swallowed hard. "I've missed you too, Bailey. So much," I whispered, placing a gentle kiss on the top of her head. "I've missed this."

I could have sat there all night with her in my arms. The second I closed my eyes was the moment she pushed away and sat up, looking down at her watch. "We should get back. Everyone's going to be wondering where we are."

I checked my watch. My escape to my room had turned into a two-hour escape. As much as I wanted to avoid the crowd of the wedding party, I nodded and stood, taking her hand in mine. We didn't say another word between us while we walked back to the hotel. The walk I had wished would last forever seemed to go by so fast, and soon I held the door open as she ducked below my arm and went inside.

We'd walked into the lobby and stopped just outside the bank of elevators where she turned toward me. I looked down into those beautiful blue eyes. The way she looked at me told me she didn't want to part ways anymore than I did. I wanted her.

"Why don't you come with me up to my room?" I asked.

She tore her eyes from mine and bit her bottom lip. "I can't, Jackson. I'm supposed to be spending the night in the bridal suite with Cara."

The disappointment that shot through me hurt almost as bad as the morning she walked out on me, but I swallowed my pride and nodded. "Well, can't blame me for trying. I guess this is good night then."

She nodded. "I guess," she said, lowering her eyes from mine.

As I stared into her eyes, I knew she didn't want to part ways. It was more the answer she felt Cara would expect her to give. I didn't want her to think I was looking for a booty call, because I wasn't. She leaned forward and pressed the button for the elevator and stepped back. That was when I placed my finger under her chin, lifting those beautiful blue eyes back to mine, leaned in, and gently placed a kiss on her lips.

"Good night," I whispered.

I heard a rumble of laughter and pulled away instantly, looking over my shoulder as the boys poured out of the lounge.

"There you are!" Ryan yelled across the lobby. "Bout time you came down here and join us losers."

I turned to see Bailey smile as she walked away from me toward the elevators. "Good luck with that. Good night. I will see you tomorrow," she said as she left me standing there as the guys made their way over to me.

# Bailey

"I now pronounce you husband and wife."

I wiped my eyes and watched as Cara and Ryan kissed. Everyone erupted into applause as they began their descent down the aisle. I was so happy to know that my best friend had found the love of her life that I could barely take my eyes off the happy couple. Cara stopped a little way down the aisle to hug family members, and Ryan was giving high fives out to a group of co-workers. It was nice to see the pair of them so happy. It was then the priest leaned into me and pointed across the aisle. I looked over to see Jackson waiting across the aisle. He held his arm out for me to take, and that was when Sierra tapped me on the shoulder and nodded in his direction.

"Bailey, we have to go." She whispered.

The look he gave me made my stomach flip. I smiled

in his direction, flipped the bouquet I was holding to my other hand, and laced my arm through his. The second I stood beside him, I could feel the heat rolling off his body. We both smiled at the crowd, and together we walked down the aisle, following the newly married couple out to the flower garden of the hotel for pictures.

Once outside, the photographer began shouting out directions. I swallowed hard. The sick feeling I'd woken with this morning was still present. Cara had asked me many times what was wrong, but I just shrugged it off as nerves.

"What do you have to be nervous about?" She laughed as we sat, I having our makeup done.

I shrugged. "I have nothing to be nervous about. You know I don't like crowds." I whispered to her so the other girls didn't hear. Then I, too, started laughing, doing my best to get myself back to normal.

I had mentioned nothing to Cara the night before about meeting Jackson in the park. I'd gone up to the spa afterward and tried to relax, but when I got to my room, the only thing I could think of was what it was like to be held by him again.

As the morning wore on, the laughter between us woman as we got ready took my mind off of everything and I was finally feeling normal again. That was until I set eyes on Jackson for the first time since we parted ways last night. The butterflies started all over again. I'd fought off nauseousness during the entire ceremony. Now, while the photographer reloaded his camera with a new card and continued taking more pictures of the bride and groom, I stood off to the side, watching the men.

Jackson stood there, talking and laughing with the guys. His eyes danced as they joked about something, and then his eyes locked with mine. Instantly, my mind went straight to last night, standing in the lobby as he leaned down and brushed his lips against mine. That kiss had sat in the forefront of my mind the entire night. That kiss had made my heart skip a beat, and it was just now that I realized I wanted to feel that kiss again.

I wanted to feel his lips against mine, his arms wrapped around me, pulling me against him. I'd had those feelings on my mind since I'd returned to Sunset Cove. It frightened me to think that almost every single night I had fallen asleep to the memory of him lying behind me, holding me the way he used to.

As the photographer shouted out new directions and continued to click away with his camera, I continued getting lost in my own thoughts. I thought about Jackson and me sitting on that park bench last night. I'd felt so safe with his arm around me. I felt so at home with my body against him, my nose buried in the nape of his neck, allowing me to smell the mixture of cologne and his scent. It had felt so good to sit with him like that, with no pressure on what was to come. It was something I hadn't felt in a long time, just to be in the moment with someone. I couldn't recall a time I'd ever felt that way with Jim. I always felt there was some expectation from him I needed to meet, but with Jackson, I always felt like I was home.

That feeling solidified the belief that Jim had been right. If we had stayed together, we would only settle for something less than we each deserved. It had taken me a while to realize that I wanted my life to be full of these electrifying moments. I wanted to feel the flutter of butterflies when my significant other looked at me. I wanted to know that I was special and know that those brief glances from across the room told me he wanted me. I wanted to feel special when he asked me out. Hell, I wanted to be made to feel wanted even when we just sat on the couch wrapped up in one another and watched a movie, wearing sweatpants and a t-shirt. I wanted to feel that anticipation again; I wanted to feel alive again, and I'd only ever felt that with Jackson.

"All right, men, it's the ladies' turn," the photographer announced, pulling me out of my thoughts.

I blinked hard and noticed that most of the men were already over where we'd been standing, and the ladies were on their way over. I was about to step away when Jackson stopped in front of me.

"Can't stop thinking of me, huh?" He smiled. "It's okay, I can tell."

I rolled my eyes and shook my head. His cockiness was

always something I'd adored, but I didn't want to let on that he was right. Instead, I slipped and gave him a small smile, which was returned with that sexy grin I loved.

Four hours later, everything to do with the wedding was done. People were on the dance floor. I stood over by the dessert counter looking for another piece of the cheesecake I'd had earlier when I felt a familiar touch on my arm. I turned to see Jackson standing there holding a plate with what appeared to be the last slice of cheesecake.

"Thought you might look for this. Would you like some?" he asked, holding the plate out to me.

I smiled. "How did you know?"

"There isn't much I don't know about you." I watched as he stuck the fork he was holding into the cheesecake, breaking off a piece. He brought the fork up and slid it slowly into my mouth, the sweet dessert sending my taste buds into overdrive.

"Has anyone ever told you that your eyes dance when you eat this stuff?" he whispered, bringing another forkful to my mouth.

I shook my head and was about to take the fork from his hand and feed him a piece when the announcement for the wedding party to have their dance came over the speaker. The slow music that played sent those same butterflies that had finally calmed in my stomach to flutter again as I looked to Jackson. He carefully set the plate down and took my hands in his, pulling me toward the dance floor.

"What are you doing?" I said, following him.

"You heard. It's time for the wedding party to dance." He grinned and then pulled me into his embrace. I was about to fight it, but the second I was in his arms, my body relaxed, and before I knew it, my head rested on his chest. I closed my eyes as we swayed to the music.

By midnight, most of the wedding party and guests were drunk. Cara and Ryan had already retired to their room for the night. I sat sipping on the last bit of my wine and watching Jackson as he talked with a couple of guys across the room. I watched as he shook hands with them, saying goodbye, and then he locked eyes with me. He made his way across the dance floor and took a seat beside me.

"You just about ready to blow this party?"

"I could use some quietness, yes."

He nodded, stood up, and held his hand out for me to take.

"Where are we going?" I questioned.

"Do you trust me?" he asked.

As he looked at me, I easily got lost in his blue eyes and nodded my head. He held his hand out for me to take.

I slid my hand into his, and we walked out of the party room and into the quietness of the hall. The longer we walked, the quieter it got, and soon we stood outside the elevator. He leaned in to press the button.

It was only a matter of seconds before the doors opened and we entered that quiet elevator together. I leaned over and hit the button for the tenth floor, and he hit the twelfth, then he turned and looked at me. My body heated at the intense look of want in his eyes as he slowly approached me, slowly wrapping his arms around me. I didn't fight. Instead, I welcomed him. He pressed me up against the mirrored walls and kissed me hard.

"Come back to my room with me. Don't turn me down two nights in a row," he pleaded as his lips left mine and danced down my neck.

I closed my eyes, trying to fight against all the things I was feeling. The feelings of want I had for this man intensified the longer he kissed me. While his hands traveled my body, the harder it became for me to deny the want I had for him. I'd barely heard the ding of the elevator, letting me know we had hit my floor. "Come with me," he whispered in my ear as he sucked my lobe between his lips.

A jolt of electricity flew through my body, and I swallowed hard, giving him a nod. There were no words spoken before he placed his lips over mine and pressed himself into me, pushing me even harder against the wall.

We'd barely made it down the hall and into his room before we'd started undressing one another. I pushed his shirt off his shoulders and pulled at his belt, fighting with the buckle, as he unzipped my dress, sliding it off my shoulders. It landed in a pile on the floor. His eyes washed over me, over the black lace bra and panty set I had purchased just for today.

His eyes hid nothing as I pulled at the button on his pants and allowed them to fall to the floor. My heart was beating so hard I felt dizzy and was glad when he took me in his arms. I almost moaned out loud when his fingers slowly traced the cup of my bra, sending chills through my body, my nipples instantly hardening beneath the fabric.

It felt as if we were barely moving. He studied my eyes and leaned in, taking my mouth with his, kissing me slower and deeper than before. I felt his hand wrap around my waist, while the other unclipped the back of my bra, the fabric falling away from my body. His lips moved from my mouth, down my neck, and continued kissing their way down my body as he pulled my bra down my arms. I rested my hands on his strong shoulders as he kneeled in front of me and looked up at me, gently pressing a kiss to my navel. The fire he held in his eyes told me I was in trouble. Running my fingers through his thick hair, he placed another kiss on my belly while he dragged my panties down. He took his time, placing gentle kisses on my hips as his fingers skimmed my legs, creating a fire in my body I could barely stand.

I stood there completely naked, his eyes washing over my body, then he stood, and his eyes locked with mine as he gently guided me over to the already turned-down bed. He slowly brought his lips to mine as we both sunk onto the mattress, his kiss turning demanding and aggressive as his hand roamed my body. I could already feel my arousal building and knew that the second he slipped his fingers between my legs, I'd shatter. As he settled over me, I could feel his arousal. I ran my hand over the large bulge in the front of his boxers, a barely audible moan escaping his throat.

I parted my legs slightly as I felt his hand run up my thigh, allowing him to run his two fingers through my slick center, drawing the lightest of circles over my clit. I moaned into his mouth as he continued swirling his finger over the sensitive bud.

I almost let out a cry as I felt my orgasm already building. I slipped my fingers into his thick hair while he trailed kisses down my neck to my heaving chest. He didn't wait. His mouth found my left nipple. He sucked it into his mouth, swirling his tongue around it, then he moved to the right, causing more shock waves than I could handle to run through my body.

"Slow down," I cried.

"I'm going slow, believe me." He breathed hard. "Just come undone for me," he whispered, as he slid down the bed, working his fingers harder and faster. "I want to watch you quiver like you used to in my arms."

I gripped his wrist, but he ignored me. Every nerve in

my body was on overdrive, and then I felt him lick and nip the inside of my thigh, and I heard myself make a sound I didn't recognize.

"That's it," he whispered and sucked my clit into his mouth. "You're so close."

I couldn't hold back any longer. It was only a matter of seconds before he had me screaming out his name as my orgasm crashed through me.

He didn't wait for me to come down. Instead, he kicked his boxers off, spread my legs, and slid himself into me, a low, feral growl leaving his lips.

"My God, you are tighter than I remember," he breathed as he continued to rock into me.

I could already feel myself climaxing again. He wrapped me in his arms and slowed his rhythm, kissing me as he thrust deeply into me. I bit my bottom lip as I felt myself tightening around him, digging my fingers into his back. He thrust deeper and faster, finally collapsing on top of me.

"Don't move," he said, breathing hard as he rolled off me.

I lay there, allowing myself to come down. The bed moved as he got up and instantly I panicked. What the hell had just happened? Something I'd promised myself wouldn't. I was about to get up and get dressed when the bed dipped and I felt his hand on my hip, pulling me into him. He placed a soft kiss on my shoulder and pulled the covers over us.

"You comfortable?" He asked, slipping his arm under my neck, his other around my waist.

"Hmmm, yes." I said, trying to let my body relax against his.

"I can't tell you how much I've missed this. How much I've missed you." He whispered, placing a soft kiss on my bare shoulder.

I closed my eyes. I wasn't sure I was ready to hear this after what had just happened. I wasn't ready because I'd missed him just as much. It was like home in his arms and no matter how much I told myself this wasn't where I was supposed to be, my body told me differently. I closed my eyes, trying to let go of the anxiety I felt, knowing what had just happened between us, and closed my eyes. One more kiss from him and a tear rolled down my cheek. I already knew I was home. I just needed to convince myself of this.

He drifted off to sleep quickly, but I lay there wide awake, worrying about what had just happened.

# Jackson

I lay in bed, my arms crossed behind my head. Last night had been the best sex and the best sleep I'd had in five years, and I regretted absolutely nothing.

Staring up at the ceiling, I wondered what sort of complications I would face in the morning when Bailey woke up. I'd woken in the middle of the night, thinking it had all been a dream, and when I found her in my arms, I silently thanked God.

Almost as if someone commanded it, my cock instantly hardened, just like it used to when we were together. I couldn't help myself. She was gorgeous as she lay there, her body wrapped around me just like before. I lay there, watching her sleep until I could no longer take it. My body was on fire as I woke her, and we'd made love for the second time that night, the third not falling far behind at just a little after five this morning. With her I was completely insatiable, and I had woken a bit ago with my hard cock pressed firmly against her ass.

I'd pulled her tighter to me, kissing the spot where her neck and shoulder met. The soft moan she let out was my undoing. In a matter of minutes, I'd slid myself into her once again and fucked her until she had screamed out my name again. Now she lay beside me, totally spent, drifting in and out of sleep while I lay here, wide awake, fearing what would happen once she realized what we'd done.

Would she be full of regret and want to leave immediately? Would she be angry at me for putting her in this position? I did not know how she was going to handle this, but I was trying to prepare myself for the worst. I was afraid that her reaction would shatter my heart once again into a million little pieces, just like she'd done before.

I closed my eyes and relaxed on the mattress, trying to calm myself. Without knowing, there was no use in getting worked up over how I was feeling. I'd just closed my eyes when I felt the bed move, and I looked over to see Bailey roll over and press herself up against me. Her warm body fit perfectly against mine and she rested her arm across my chest. A couple minutes later she looked up at me with sleep-filled eyes. I could see the want in them, and I slid my arm under her neck, pulling her against me.

"Morning," she murmured as she rested her head on my shoulder, her fingers drawing circles on my chest.

"Good morning." I adjusted myself, pulling her closer still, wrapping her in my arms, and bringing a kiss to her forehead.

She was quiet. I looked down at her fingers as she traced over the sensitive scar on my chest.

"Where did you get this?" she asked as she ran her finger over the raised skin. "You never had that before." She whispered.

I looked down into those big blue eyes of hers, unsure if I should tell her or not. I knew exactly how she felt about my job, especially after Connor had died. I could remember the nights when she'd begged me to do something else, anything else after he'd been killed. The anxiety she'd felt was almost paralyzing for her and it killed me to know she was in that state every time I left the house. I cleared my throat. There was no way I was going to hide it, I thought, because being a cop was in my blood. It was who I was. Just like it had been in her brother's blood. No matter what she said, I would never change.

"It happened during an arrest a couple of years ago. We took down a couple of guys. Even though we'd searched them both, we missed the knife the one guy had. My partner was busy loading the other into the car and while I went to cuff the other, he pulled a knife on me. We struggled, and he ended up hitting me in the vest. The knife went right through the plate. Thankfully, that was when backup arrived."

I prepared myself for the backlash, but she didn't say anything. She was quiet and continued to run her finger over the raised scar. I pulled her closer to me, placing another kiss on her forehead.

"It looks worse than what it was." I said, trying to ease her anxiety. Something I was so used to doing. It was second nature. "It took about ten stitches, that was it. No major damage was done, but it left this nice little reminder."

"Did it hurt?" She questioned.

"Maybe a little. I think the stitches hurt more." I chuckled, pressing my lips to her forehead.

"You lie."

"I don't lie. They really did hurt more. I barely even felt the knife. My adrenaline was so high."

We lay there quietly for a few moments. She continued to run her fingers over that scare while I looked into her eyes. When she stopped, I propped myself up on my elbow and rolled her onto her back and slowly brought my lips to hers. I could feel myself already growing harder the slower and deeper I kissed her.

When our lips parted, she looked up at me, worry in her eyes despite the smile on her lips. "Jackson, as fun as last night was, I really should get back to my room."

I felt as if I'd run into a cement wall. These were not the words I wanted to hear. I calmed my beating heart and cleared my throat. "Why?" I questioned.

"Come on, Jackson. We have brunch in a couple of hours. I need to get ready. Plus, the girls will come to meet me, and I showed up here alone. I really should be in my room when they do."

I couldn't help but feel a little crushed that she would be embarrassed about being with me. Instead of letting her words get to me, I decided I was going to fight for this. "So? What would be so wrong with you not being in your room when they came to get you? Instead of going with them, would it be so bad if we went to brunch together?"

Bailey let out a breath and looked away from me. "Jackson, we can't do this."

"We can't do what?"

"This, we can't do this. We can't show up together." She said, sitting up and pulling the blankets around her to cover her naked body.

"Are you embarrassed to be with me?" I questioned, getting up from the bed.

"No, it's not that." She answered, her voice weak.

"Then what is it?"

"We just can't do this."

"We can't do what? What is 'this'?" I asked, watching and waiting for her to answer me.

"This...us, in front of our friends." She buried her face in her hands. "I'm not ready to let them know. I was barely ready for this, for what happened between us last night and again this morning."

I sat back down and looked at her. "Well, this has already happened." I said, my fingers dancing along the skin of her hip.

"Yes, I know...but..."

"But what? All we're going to be doing is showing up to brunch together."

Bailey looked from me to the window and sat there quietly for a few minutes before turning back to me. "Jackson, I'm..."

"You're what?"

"I'm not ready to date you." Bailey scrambled out from under me, this time grabbing the blanket off the end of the bed, holding it against her chest.

"Why? Give me one good reason why not, because ever since you've been back in town, I've been getting nothing but those messages from you."

"What? How do you figure?"

"Come on, Bailey. Do you really need to ask me that? How about all the late-night text messages, the need to feel protected when you are at work with Marcus? You weren't calling Cara or one of the other girls. You were calling me."

"Seriously? The late-night text messages were about the wedding, nothing else." She said, turning away from me and walked to the window where she stood looking out.

I grabbed my sweatpants from the chair in the corner

and threw them on. "Sure. Whatever you say."

"What is that supposed to mean?"

"Bailey, the texting may have started out being about the wedding. But when we were still messaging at four in the morning about nonsense bullshit, flirting back and forth, I'd say it's more than 'just about a wedding."

She turned around and glared at me, saying nothing, because in her heart she knew I was right, and I knew she knew it. The second she got defensive with the high-pitched tone, she knew I'd called her on her bullshit.

"Trust me, it was about the wedding."

I met her eyes and shook my head. "Whatever you say." I shrugged and dialed room service. I ordered two coffees to be sent up to my room, ignoring the fact that she was planning on leaving. Once finished, I turned back to her. She now sat back on the edge of the bed, looking at me, but saying nothing.

"I see you're at a loss for words because you know I am right."

She swallowed hard and looked up at me. "Fine, maybe there were a couple of nights I might have been flirting with you."

"A couple of nights? Are you fucking kidding me right now? Do I need to show you our messages? It was every fucking night, Bailey, for two straight weeks."

"What are you talking about?" she bit out, pulling the covers higher against her chest.

I reached for my phone and pulled up one of our last conversations, handing it to her. She reluctantly took the phone from me, her eyes wandering over the messages we'd exchanged. Then she handed it back to me. "I see nothing wrong with it." She shrugged.

"Really?" I looked down at the message and started reading it aloud.

Bailey: "Do you ever think about us?"

Jackson: "Of course. Do you?"

Bailey: "Yes, often."

Jackson: "More often now, then before?"

Bailey: "Yes."

Jackson: "What do you think about?"

Bailey: "All things. You?"

Jackson: "Come on, Bailey, be more specific. What sort of things?"

Bailey: "I don't know if I should tell you.

Jackson: You most definitely should tell me.

> Bailey: :/ If I must tell you, right now I am wishing you were here. Laying behind me with your arms wrapped around me so I could sleep again.

I looked over my phone and met her eyes as I finished reading the message out loud.

"I'd had a few drinks."

I scrolled down through the messages. "Did you have a few drinks when you sent me this?" I questioned, showing her the image on my phone. Her cheeks flushed, and she buried her face in her hands when she saw the picture of herself wearing a black bra and panty set that left nothing to the imagination. "You can't tell me for one second that this was about the fucking wedding."

"It totally was. I wore that the night of the rehearsal dinner."

"Is that so? I certainly didn't see it. It's a shame you covered it up." I said, glaring at her.

Finally, she broke my stare, and her eyes lowered to the floor. "Fine, you're right, I was flirting, but that doesn't mean I am ready for the pressure of a relationship with you."

"What pressure? I've never pressured you into anything. Ever." I answered, raising my voice.

"I'm not ready for the pressure of everyone knowing. I'm not ready to hear it from our friends, or from my mother. Do you know I'd been in Sunset Cove less than thirty hours when someone saw me downtown by the station? In a matter of minutes, they'd already called my mother to ask if we were back together. Not to mention, my mother has barely stopped bringing up your name since the morning you brought me home."

I watched as her chest rose and fell in rapid succession as she sat there watching me. I could see the panic in her eyes. I sat down beside her and placed my hand on her cheek.

"Bailey, no one needs to know. We keep this between us for a little while, to see how things go. We work on us and only us."

She shook her head. "I don't know," she muttered.

"The only pressure that will be there is the pressure you put on yourself. Other than that, there will be none. We can keep it quiet, just between us. We can put all the old shit behind us and just focus on things between us with no outside influence. That way, if we don't work out, we aren't hurting anyone else. We just go our separate ways."

"Are you suggesting we sneak around like a couple of kids?"

I shrugged. I did not know what I was suggesting. But if it meant that I got to work on another chance with the woman I knew I still loved, then I would do damn near anything. "I guess maybe I am."

Bailey was quiet. I could tell she was thinking about

what I'd suggested. A knock on the door tore me away from those gorgeous blue eyes, and I wandered over and took the two cups of coffee from the guy. When I returned to the bedside, Bailey sat there with a small smile on her face.

"Here," I said, handing her the cup of hot coffee.

"Thank you." She took the mug from my hand and took a sip, then looked at me. "Do you think we could do that?" she asked as I sat down beside her.

"What, sneak around? I don't see why we couldn't. It would make me feel like I'm fifteen again. Remember when I used to sneak into your bedroom window at two in the morning to screw around?" I asked, raising my eyebrows in gest.

"Oh God, don't remind me of that." She giggled, a light blush coming to her cheeks. "I still can't believe that no one heard us."

"I know." I chuckled. "I always worried about meeting your mother in the morning, holding a knife, ready to chop my dick off. I'll tell you, by the time I'd get to the front door, my shirt was soaked from sweat."

"Mom wouldn't have done that." She giggled.

"Never know. However, I am pretty sure your brother may have heard us because a couple of weeks later, he mentioned something to me. Now he would have chopped my dick off." I chuckled as I thought back to the memory of that night. It was the first time we'd had sex. I could remember kissing her and telling her to be quiet because her brother had been asleep on the other side of the wall and her mother was just down the hall.

"Oh my God, are you serious?" she said, burying her face in her hands once again. "I'm glad you never told me before. I'd of never been able to look him in the face."

"Why do you think I didn't tell you that until now?"

"Jackson!" She giggled, taking a sip of her coffee, then shaking her head in disbelief.

I smiled and then took a sip of my hot coffee. "I say we start at brunch. I think we could go together but pretend to run into each other just outside of the room, and we go in together. We can sit together as well."

"I don't know, Jackson. They are going to know."

I shook my head. "No, they won't."

Bailey looked at me, completely unconvinced, but still held that curious little smile on her face. I'd always found that smile so adorable when she thought I was being totally ridiculous.

"They will know." She repeated. "They will know because I made a deal out of everything whenever it came to you."

I met her eyes. "Well now, that was just a silly thing to do, but don't worry about it." I winked. "They won't know."

"All right, we will try it your way, but when they know, I'm sending them to you," Bailey answered.

# Bailey

I shut the water off and stepped out of the shower. I grabbed the towel that hung on the hook and wrapped myself up in the plush terry cloth. I felt sick to my stomach. Why had I agreed to this ridiculousness that Jackson had proposed?

I looked at myself in the mirror and swallowed hard. I even looked sick, and I knew that the second Cara looked at me, she'd know something was up. I looked at myself one more time, took a deep breath and grabbed another towel, this time drying my hair.

It was no use; she'd take one look at me, and I'd have to tell her everything. I looked less stressed than I had in years. I looked at peace. He'd had his hands on me one night, one night, and he'd done this. I glanced at the clock on the nightstand. I didn't have much time. I reached for my cell phone and typed a message to Jackson, then stopped and re-read it. My finger hovered over the send button, my stomach rolled and without even thinking another thought, I deleted the message.

I walked over to the closet and pulled out the outfit I'd brought for this morning.

"Damn him." I muttered to myself.

I was just about to return to the bathroom when my cell phone vibrated on the bed. I glanced over to see a message from Cara there. I grabbed my phone, hoping and praying that he may be my way out of going to brunch with Jackson.

> CARA: Hey, sorry to do this. We are going to be a little late this morning ;) Last night was just a little too good (if you catch my drift)

I shook my head. My stomach was now rolling with nerves. I got her message loud and clear and swallowed hard as I thought about my night in paradise.

> CARA: Don't you have anything to say to that ;)

> BAILEY: Stop your bragging. ;)

I smiled and threw my phone down on the bed, only to see another message pop up.

> CARA: Not bragging. Speaking facts.
> You be okay to get there on your own.

> BAILEY: Sure, I'll find it. I'm a big girl.
> ;) Take your time.

> CARA: We will. Just heading to the
> shower now ;)

> BAILEY: Oh gross. I don't want all the
> meaty details.

> CARA: Well, I do…going to stuff his
> salami inside of me now.

My face heated at her comment. I'd never be able to look at Ryan the same way now. I threw my phone down on the bed and was about to head into the bathroom to do my hair and makeup when someone knocked on my door.

I didn't think about the towel I was wearing, and pulled the door open without checking who it was first. It was then I met his blue eyes as they danced down my towel clad body.

"If you don't want them to wonder what's up, I think you may want to put on a little more." He winked.

"Sorry, I didn't think you'd be here already. I just got out of the shower and was about to get dressed…"

"It's okay. I was ready, so I thought I'd just come up

here and keep you company. May I come in?" He said, leaning against the door frame, reaching out and gently tugging on my towel.

I stepped to the side and let him in, shutting the door behind him. "Now if you'll excuse me."

His eyes followed me as I walked into the bathroom and shut the door behind me. I looked at myself in the mirror, my cheeks red with embarrassment.

With my makeup and hair done, I once again stepped out of the bathroom, still wrapped in my towel, and met eyes with Jackson, who sat over on the chair in my room. He looked relaxed and intently watched me as I grabbed my clothes from the bed.

"You don't need to go into the bathroom. It's not like I didn't see everything last night." He said, giving me a sexy smile.

I shook my head and almost melted on the spot as his eyes met mine. The hint of playfulness in his eyes told me that if I changed in front of him, we'd never get to brunch on time. We also wouldn't beat Cara and Ryan, and that was what I needed to do to pull this off.

I grabbed my stuff and was just about to the bathroom when I felt the towel I'd had wrapped around me slip. I jerked around and came face to face with Jackson, who stood before me, his hands now resting on my bare hip. His look was so intense, his touch was so soft, I could already feel my arousal. He didn't give me a chance. Almost immediately, his lips were on mine.

I dropped the clothes I held in my hand and wrapped my arms around his neck, his tongue washing through my mouth. He wrapped his arms around me and kissed me harder while his other hand found its way into my thick hair.

My body betrayed me as I felt my arousal growing stronger and a soft moan escaped my lips as his lips pressed against mine, harder this time. I rested my hands on his chest, my fingers finding the buttons on his shirt. He let me go and tugged at his shirt, pulling it out of his pants, while I shoved his shirt off his broad strong shoulders, then I moved to his belt.

A couple of tugs, and one swift movement from him and his pants were on the ground. He stepped out of them, picked me up and carried me over to my bed, laying me down. He kissed the top of my breasts, then his mouth found my hardened nipple. Sucking the one into his mouth, while I cupped his balls, and ran my hand over his hard cock.

"God, I've wanted you for so long." He mumbled, going back and forth between my nipples, sucking them into his mouth just hard enough to feel him in the pit of my stomach. I bit my bottom lip and ran my hand up his bicep to his shoulder, everything in me telling me I should stop him. I was about to say his name when he reached between my legs and ran his finger through my slick, throbbing center.

He dropped to his knees, his hands traveling to my hips, while he kissed the inside of each thigh. The stubble on his face tickled against the sensitive skin of my inner thighs. He took the skin of my thighs between his teeth, giving me a soft love bite right before connecting his tongue to my center.

One lick, one strong lick over that little bundle of nerves, and I was ready to hit the roof. I let out a loud moan as he continued his glorious torture.

"God, Jackson..." I hissed, letting my head fall back while I arched my back off the bed as he continued delivering firm licks over the swollen bundle of nerves.

He dug his fingers into my hips and sucked me into his mouth, his tongue now circling me. I bit my bottom lip to keep from screaming as my orgasm built.

"Don't keep quiet for me. I want to hear you." He whispered, before he lowered his mouth back to my center.

My eyes closed tight, my back arched off the bed. I slipped my fingers into his thick hair and let out a loud moan that filled the room. "Jackson...please..."

He didn't let up, instead keeping one hand on my hip, I felt him press two fingers at my opening, sliding them inside of me just enough that I knew he was there. A few minutes of him tracing around my opening, he slipped his fingers deep inside of me, his tongue dancing over my clit, only this time he wasn't stopping. He picked up the pace and soon I was writhing on the bed screaming his name.

I'd barely had a moment to come down when I felt him flip me on the bed and pull me up onto my knees. He gripped my shoulder, pushing me down onto the bed, and slid his hard cock deep inside of me. I was so tight and felt so full as he thrust into me.

"God Bailey. You feel so amazing." He hissed, as he pounded into me at a quick fast pace.

I fisted the sheets and closed my eyes tight while I allowed myself to feel every inch of him. I reached down and cupped his already tight balls, cradling them. He'd always loved it when I did that and the second my hand connected with him, his breathing changed. A few seconds later, his body tight as he gave the last few thrusts, before letting his release take over his body.

I pressed the button for the elevator and stood back, fidgeting with my small clutch purse as I looked at my watch.

"Bailey, relax." Jackson said quietly while watching me.

"I can't. We are late."

"So what? We're late. Big deal. So everyone has to wait a few minutes longer to eat."

"It matters, Jackson. I spoke to Cara over an hour ago. I told her I would be up shortly."

Jackson let out a breath and stepped over to me, wrapping his arm around my waist. "Relax." He whispered, his breath tickling my neck as his lips danced over my skin. "You're plans...they changed." He said, rubbing his nose along the column of my neck, taking in the scent of my perfume.

"Stop. This is the exact actions that got us to this point."

"So what?" He whispered, wrapping his arms around the front of my body, resting them on my stomach, his fingers dancing lightly over my bare skin. "A little trouble is good for everyone." He said, nipping my earlobe.

My stomach twisted and suddenly I felt sick. I wasn't ready for this. I wasn't ready to answer questions about us. I wasn't ready for him to be all over me, yet here we were.

"I thought I explained myself to you earlier this morning." I said, closing my eyes as I leaned against him.

"You did, and I respect that. I swear they won't even notice."

The ding of the elevator tore me from his arms and together we stepped inside. I'd never be so happy to see another person inside of the elevator because that meant that he would have to keep his hands occupied. I stepped over to the far corner of the elevator and waited while Jackson hit the floor number.

The instant the door opened, I stepped out and walked ahead of Jackson down the hall to the room where our brunch was being held. I stopped just outside the door, ran my hand over my hair and looked down and ran my hands over my pants, hoping to smooth them out. I took a deep breath and then rounded the corner. Everyone was seated at the table and the second I stepped inside; they all turned their eyes on me and then they fell on the man behind me. Immediately, all talking silenced, and they all stared in our direction.

I noticed immediately that Cara and Ryan gave one another a knowing glance, and then Ryan stood up and cleared his throat. "Well, there they are. We were about to send out a search party." He said, coming over and guiding me to an empty chair. The second I sat down he turned and shook hands with Jackson and mumbled something to him I could quite make out.

Cara leaned over to me and placed her hand on mine. "Everything okay?" she questioned, glancing over at Jackson and then at me.

My stomach rolled, and I reached for the glass of water in front of me. My hand shook as I took a sip and then nodded. Jackson pulled out the chair beside me and sat down.

"Morning Cara." He said, ignoring the fact that she was waiting for me to respond. "Sorry to keep everyone waiting."

"Morning Jackson. No worries." She answered and then looked at me. "Bailey?" She whispered, "Is everything okay?"

I nodded my head because I knew if I spoke, my voice would give everything away. I brought my water glass to my mouth and took another sip, swallowing hard.

I was sure she'd turn her attention to Ryan while we waited for food, but she didn't. Instead, she kept her eyes trained on me. "You sure everything is fine?" She asked again. "You look...odd."

I nodded, "I'm fine." I whispered, my voice cracking. She squinted her eyes as if she were trying to read me, but I looked away. I was never so glad when Ryan started talking to the entire table, finally taking Cara's eyes from me.

Ryan said a few words while our food was being served. When the server placed my breakfast in front of me, my stomach rolled at the smell of my egg omelet. I hated lying to my best friend, and I knew she'd take one look at my pale face and she'd know exactly what had happened.

"Be a good girl and eat your breakfast." Jackson whispered in my ear as his hand slid onto my upper thigh, gently squeezing it. I just about jumped up from where I was sitting when I casually glanced in his direction. He gave me a tiny nod, then leaned over and whispered into my ear.

"Calm yourself. Don't worry, everything is fine. They don't know."

When I looked up from where I'd been staring down at my plate, I noticed Cara watching me with a curious look and it was at that moment I knew she knew.

# Bailey

A Week Later

I sat on the couch in the living room watching TV when my mother emerged from her bedroom all dressed and ready to go to the gardening club meeting.

"Where are you going?" I asked, looking over at her.

"I'm so sorry, dear. I have to go out tonight. I just feel awful about this. Especially since this is really the first night you have been home since you returned," she said as she stood in front of the mirror and put a coat of lipstick on.

"Seriously, Mom, don't worry about me. I'll be fine."

"You could always come with me. It would be nice to spend an evening with my daughter. We can go talk about plants, and then we could go for coffee and some cake afterward. A little mother daughter date."

Gardening wasn't really my thing, and Mom knew it. The last thing I wanted to do was talk about plants with a bunch of people I didn't know. "It's okay, Mom. I have snacks and drinks here, not to mention there are some great movies on TV tonight."

"I know, it's just, I've missed you so," she said, turning to look at me. "It was a terrible night for this seminar." She mumbled.

"Seriously, mom, it's okay. Go learn about your gardenias. We can have a mother daughter date another night. I'll probably hit the sack early, anyway."

Mom turned and looked at me with an annoyed look on her face. "It's poinsettias. Tonight's seminar is on poinsettias, not gardenias. Never mind, you'd probably be bored to death, anyway. You don't even like plants."

I let out a giggle. Mom looked flustered and I couldn't help but laugh. She had only been talking about this meeting all week. "I know it's about poinsettias, Mom. I was just messing with you."

"Bailey." She met my eyes.

I got up off the couch and walked over to the door. "Have a good night, okay? You'll be back, what, at ten?"

"Probably closer to eleven. Susan and I always go for coffee afterward. Although maybe I will just tell her we can do that another night. Yeah, that is exactly what I'll do."

"No, mom, it's fine, really. Go talk poinsettias, then go have coffee and cake. I'll be here watching *Eat, Pray, Love, stuffing my face full of pizza* and popcorn. Like I said, I'll probably turn in early. I am tired. The wedding events took a toll on me, all those late nights."

"Okay. Well, enjoy your movie and pizza." Mom said, leaning in and kissing me on the cheek.

"I will." I smiled while guiding her to the door and shutting it behind her.

I watched through the window as Mom climbed into her car and reversed out of the driveway and drove off down the road. I locked the front door and went back to my corner of the sofa, pulling the large plush blanket up over my legs. It was snowy, a great night to stay in and curl up on the couch. The credits had just started when my phone vibrated. I shoved a handful of popcorn in my mouth and looked down at the screen, a small smile appearing on my lips as Jackson's name flashed.

"Hey," I said, answering the phone.

"What are you doing?"

"I just settled on the couch. Going to watch *Eat Pray Love.*"

"I have a better option. How would you like to go to the movies with me?"

I smiled to myself. He sounded nervous, and I found that to be adorable.

"Sounds great, but just one question."

"What would that be?" his deep voice rumbled.

"Well, if we are secretly dating, then how are we going to go to the movies together?"

Jackson chuckled, "Well, we just meet inside."

I thought for a second and smiled to myself. "So, wait a minute. You're asking me to the movies, and I am going to have to pay for my ticket?" I suppressed the laugh I could feel coming on and tried to continue to be serious.

Jackson let out a deep sigh. "Well, Bailey, you tell me. If you want to meet out front and walk in with me like a normal couple, then I will pay. If not, then yes, you'll have to pay for your own ticket."

I crinkled my nose. He was going to beat me at my game. I cleared my throat. "What did you want to see?"

"Your choice."

I quickly looked up what was playing and chose the newest romantic comedy. "All right, I will meet you there," I said, kicking the blanket off my lap.

I'd been standing in line at the theater for close to twenty minutes when I felt a tap on my shoulder. I turned around to see Jackson standing there holding two tickets. He flashed that sexy smile and saying nothing; he held out his hand for me to take, and I climbed over the separator rope.

He leaned in and placed a kiss on my cheek. "You didn't actually think I would make you buy your own ticket, did you?"

I couldn't help but laugh. "Perhaps." I shrugged.

"Come on, let's go grab a seat." He chuckled as he wrapped his arm around me, leading us toward the theater rooms.

I placed my hand on his firm chest, our lips parting just in time for the lights to come on. I closed my eyes, trying to regain my composure. We'd been going at it for the last hour and a half, in the last row of the theater. Neither of us had seen an ounce of that movie.

"What did you think of the movie?" he asked, adjusting himself before his lips returned to mine.

"What movie?" I whispered, kissing him back.

I jumped at the sound of someone clearing their throat and looked down to see the cleaning crew. "Guess that's our cue," Jackson chuckled.

"Oh my god, I want to die." I murmured as I laughed. We walked hand in hand down the stairs and exited the theater.

We moved our way through the crowd of people who

were arriving for the next showing. Jackson pushed the door open, and we both made our way into the cool night.

The cool night air felt good on my hot, flushed skin. It gave me enough time to calm down just as we got to his car, where he slid his arm around my waist. He pushed me up against my car and pressed his lips to mine, his hands traveling to my hips, gently squeezing.

"Any chance I could convince you to come home with me?" he whispered, kissing me once more, before trailing kisses down my neck. "Where we could continue where we left off?"

"You might be able to persuade me to follow you," I whispered as I closed my eyes and his lips met mine once again. There was no use denying what I wanted. I wanted him.

Jackson wasted no time after he had locked the door behind us. I had just slipped out of my shoes when he pushed me up against the wall, kissing me so hard I could barely breathe. He undid the buttons of my blouse, slipping it off my shoulders. It fell to the floor as he kissed me again. Lifting me so I could wrap my legs around his waist, he began walking with me in his arms down to his bedroom, where he placed me down gently on the ground. His hands moved to the clasp on my bra, and with one swift motion, his fingers flicked it open, my bra falling away from my body.

I pulled at his shirt and slipped it off over his head. He stood there while I ran my hands over his hard abs, before he wrapped me in his arms and devoured my mouth once again. My skin pebbled as his hands trailed down to the button of my jeans. One quick movement was all it took and now he was slowly inching them down my legs until they pooled at my feet.

He took his time, kissing his way down my body. It only took a couple of minutes before my legs were too weak to hold myself up and we fell onto the bed together. He leaned on his forearm, bending to take my lips again, his other hand sliding inside my panties, then running through my slick heat, causing me to moan into his mouth.

"That's it." He whispered, meeting my lips again as he slid two fingers deep inside of me, his thumb circling my clit.

"I always loved how responsive you were," he whispered as his lips parted from mine. He continued to run his thumb over that small bundle of nerves while he pumped two fingers deep inside of me. I could feel the blush rising to my cheeks as our eyes met.

I placed my hand on his to stop him from continuing and tried hard to reach into his boxers and stroke him.

"No, baby, not until you come," he said, ignoring the fact that I was gripping his wrist as tight as I could to stop or at least slow him down.

I was so close, and the more his fingers danced over the sensitive bud, the harder it was becoming for me to hold back. He bent down and sucked my nipple into his mouth while his two fingers worked in and out of me. My back arched off the bed. I felt myself tighten, and I let go, calling out his name.

"That's it, baby." He whispered, kissing my mouth hard before he climbed between my legs. "God, I've been waiting all week to hear you, to feel you again."

I was dizzy from my release. I felt him run his cock through my wetness and ever so quickly slip inside of my tight heat. His hands held my hips, holding me close as he pounded into me. Each thrust he delivered getting deeper and harder until I couldn't take it anymore and began once again to tighten around him.

"I can't hold back much longer," he breathed. "But before I do, I want you to come again."

I gripped his back, digging my nails into him. It was like I was under his command. He'd said those magic words, and I came undone for the second time. In a matter of seconds, he, too, let go and emptied himself into me, collapsing on the bed beside me.

Something woke me, and I lay staring out the window of Jackson's bedroom, the light from the street falling through the slats of the blinds. Everything was silent, and I smiled to myself and snuggled down under the covers, breathing in the scent of the man who lay beside me. I was just about asleep when I felt the bed jerk.

I rolled over and looked at Jackson, who lay beside me, covered in a sheen of sweat. The look on his face wasn't restful. He looked full of torment as his head flopped side to side. I lay and watched him for a few minutes, remembering the nightmares he used to have right after Connor had died. I wondered if that was what he was dreaming about. I was just about to reach over and touch him gently to wake him when he seemed to calm down. I watched him for a few more minutes. I rolled back over and closed my eyes to go back to sleep when the thrashing started again, followed by a low growling sound.

"I tried. I tried," he repeated, his voice full of sorrow. "Sorry, I tried." He whimpered.

I rolled back over in time to see the torment lining his face. I was about to put my hand on his chest and try to wake him when he started yelling for help. I placed my hand on his chest and lowered my head onto his shoulder and quietly whispered in his ear, just like I used to do.

"Jackson, you're safe. I'm here."

Instantly, he quieted, and he wrapped his arms around me, a whimper escaping his throat as his chest heaved. "I'm sorry, I tried," he murmured as I lay in his arms. Finally, his breathing calmed, and he fell back into a deep sleep. Yet now I lay awake, tormented by the thoughts of what he had been dreaming about.

A tear escaped my eyes as I listened to his breathing. I took comfort in feeling the slow rise and fall of his chest, and being held in his arms soon outweighed my torment, and soon I too drifted off to sleep.

I woke up early the next morning. Jackson was still sound asleep, so I slipped out from under the covers, pulled his bathrobe from the hook on the back of the door, and wrapped myself in his scent. I made my way to the kitchen, where I put on a pot of coffee and sat down to check my phone to see if I had any messages.

Just the usual from my mom, worried about me not being at home when she woke this morning. I sat there debating if I should just tell her I was at Jackson's. I typed out the message and re-read it back to myself; only to realize I still wasn't ready to let anyone know that Jackson and I had been messing around. So, I deleted all the words and quickly typed back that I had spent the night at Cara's.

"Morning," I heard a sleep-filled deep voice behind me and felt his large hands on my shoulders. I reached up and held them both, while he bent down and placed a kiss on the side of my neck.

"Morning. I put some coffee on."

"Perfect." He kissed my lips and then went over to the cupboard and pulled out two mugs. "Sleep well?"

"I did, yes. What about you?"

"Like a baby." He winked and set a full, steaming mug of coffee in front of me and leaned in for another morning kiss.

It was on the tip of my tongue to ask him about the dream he'd been having, but I thought twice. What if he didn't remember it at all? What if he remembered it and didn't want to tell me? What if he was too embarrassed to talk about it? After all, I could be totally wrong about what he was dreaming of, and if I was, I wondered if it would lead to another fight. So, instead of asking, I shrugged it off instead and smiled when he pulled down a box of pancake mix and held it in his hand, turning to look at me. "You've got batter duty," he said, smiling.

I nodded, got up from the chair I was sitting on, and went to work while he cooked the bacon.

# Jackson

We hiked along the entire beach, now running to the car to warm up. Afterward, we drove to the grocery store to pick up food for dinner. I had just pulled my truck into my driveway and cut the engine when I looked over at Bailey, who flashed me a sexy smile.

"Are you hungry?" I asked.

"Am I hungry? Yes! I can't wait to bite into those steaks we picked up," she said, hopping out of the truck and grabbing the bag of food we'd picked up after we left the beach.

"Well, then let's get inside, and I will get the barbecue fired up."

Hand in hand, we ran up the walkway to the front door and into the house. "I'll get our sweatshirts into the wash while you do that," she said, running back out the front door.

I couldn't help but watch as she ran down the driveway back to the truck to grab our wet gear. I held the door open for her and she smiled, stopping to place a kiss on my lips before running off toward the laundry area. I shut and locked the door and headed into the kitchen to first season the steaks and then turn the barbecue on.

After we ate, we both showered together and then we curled up on the couch and put a movie on. She curled up to my side, resting her head on my chest, and pulled the blanket down off the back of the couch, covering us up. As the movie played, I could barely stop the thoughts running through my mind. Having her here, having her back, felt like we were becoming serious again. Since the wedding, we had spent almost all our free time together, and even though we had been apart for five years, it felt as if we had never been apart at all.

I ran my fingers through her soft hair as the credits rolled. "So, are you ever going to tell me what you have been up to for the last five years?" I questioned.

She paused and swallowed hard. "You don't want to know that, Jackson," she pushed herself up into a sitting position and rubbed her eyes.

"Sure, I do. I wouldn't ask if I didn't want to know."

She looked at me. I could tell she was trying to read me, to see if I was indeed serious or if I was just trying to get information out of her. Then she sunk back onto the couch and met my eyes.

"Well, you know I moved away from here. I had a job and started dating a guy I worked with. His name was Jim."

"Jim, huh?" I felt a wave of jealousy run through me at the thought of another man putting his hands on her.

"I told you, Jackson, you don't want to know."

"Well, while I sit here and pretend, I am not jealous, how about you tell me what happened to him?"

Bailey looked at me, rolled her eyes and let out this cute, annoyed laugh. "Well, if you must know, he dumped me on our anniversary."

I looked over at her and couldn't help the small smile that crept onto my lips.

"What's so funny about that?" she asked, defensive.

I chuckled to myself. "Well, on one hand, I think the guy is an ass for letting you go, but on the other, it was the best decision he ever made."

"What?" she said, her voice full of annoyance.

She was too cute when she got angry.

"Sorry, I can't help myself. See, if you were with him now, you wouldn't be here with me."

"Oh." Bailey giggled.

"What really happened?"

"Seriously, I think we just fell out of love, or perhaps

he never loved me to begin with. Either way, it's over. He's moved on, and here I sit."

"I see, and what about you?" I questioned.

"What about me what?"

"Have you moved on?" I held my breath and waited patiently for her answer. Her eyes met mine, and she nodded. Relief washed over me. "I'm glad. It would be awkward with Jim sitting here."

Bailey looked over at me and began laughing. "You think."

"I don't need to think. I know."

As our eyes met, the silence between us grew until finally Bailey cleared her throat. "Can I tell you something?"

"Please."

"When Cara begged me to come back, I really didn't have a reason to say no, except for you." She hung her head and clasped her hands together.

"Me?"

"Part of me was afraid of what I would find."

"How so?"

"Deep down, I was afraid I would come back and find you had gotten married, and that you'd have a family. I don't know, it's stupid."

"I see. Well, if you want to know what it is I've been up to, all you have to do is ask," I said, reaching over and brushing a strand of hair out of her eyes.

"I already know, so spare me the details," she whispered, raising her eyes to meet mine.

"What do you know?"

"Everything. Cara told me you've been doing the entire town. I don't need to hear it again, it's okay. It doesn't matter. It's not like we were together, but Zoe? Really?"

I didn't know how to respond to what Cara had told her. It wasn't like I was hiding anything, but to tell her all of that made me sound like a horrible person.

"Bailey, she makes me sound like a monster."

"No, she doesn't."

"She does. It wasn't what I was going to say at all."

"What were you going to say?"

I cleared my throat, praying that what I would have said didn't come off sounding like a line. "Well, I'd planned to tell you I'd spent the last five years waiting for you. That I'm happy to have you back in my arms." I shifted uncomfortably in my seat. "As for Zoe, she was nothing but a moment of weakness and terrible judgment."

"It doesn't matter, Jackson. If you like Zoe, it's okay because we aren't together?" Her eyes met mine, and even though her comment stung, I held her gaze. "I don't know what this is going on between us, but it's definitely not us getting back together."

"Bailey, you may be upset that I slept with 'the entire

town' as Cara put it, but it's different now. Just so you know, I ended things with Zoe a while ago. Besides, it's different with you and always has been."

I kept my eyes locked with hers. I wanted to lean in and kiss her, take her down to the bedroom and show her, just like I did last night, how different everything was with her for me. Yet I didn't dare make a move, not yet. I could already see the hurt, the tears forming in her eyes.

"I'm not upset, Jackson. You were a free man to do whatever it was you wanted," she mumbled as she looked down at her watch. "I should get going."

"Why?" I questioned.

"Because it's late, and I think, I just, I need to be alone. Besides, Mom has been alone for a couple of days, and I go back to work tomorrow through the rest of the weekend. It will be busy, I'm sure."

"So you'll be working this weekend?" I hadn't wanted to bring it up, but this coming up December weekend was the weekend Connor had died. Neither of us had mentioned anything about him since we'd been together, yet we both knew the subject hung in the air between us.

She turned her eyes away from me and nodded. She was quiet as she stared off into the corner of the room. I was sure I caught a glimmer of a tear in the corner of her eye. I was about to lean forward and ask if she was going to be okay? If she wanted me there but she put her hand on mine.

"What were you dreaming about the other night?" she questioned, her voice weak.

I knew exactly what I had been dreaming about. I'd felt her touch me when she took the time to comfort me until I fell back asleep. It was the same dream I'd had before. We were alone in that dark alley. Connor lay dead before me. Everyone had disappeared, and then he sat up and blamed me for our breakup.

"It was nothing," I lied.

She was quiet for another minute before letting out a loud sigh. "I see nothing has changed. Still not going to be truthful with me, are you?" She stood up from where she'd been sitting. "It's been five years, and you still can't tell me the truth about those dreams."

I jumped up from where I was sitting. "Bailey, what is that supposed to mean? I've always been honest with you.
"

She had just reached for her freshly washed sweatshirt that hung on the hook beside the door, her hand resting on the fabric. She said nothing for a moment or two, and then slowly turned to me. "You still can't tell me you dream of him. You had nightmares almost every single night after it happened. Yet you would never talk to me. You want things to be different, you want us back together, you need to talk to me," she said, stepping closer and jabbing her finger roughly into my chest.

"What do you want me to tell you? That you ripped

my heart out when you blamed me for his death? Do you want to know that I'm haunted by what happened and have been for the past five years? Do you need to know that every year the dreams run rampant for weeks, sometimes months, and that there is little I can do to stop them?"

Bailey looked at me with tears lining her eyes. "Jackson, I just want you to talk to me. That's all I ever wanted. I do not know why you felt you couldn't. I know in your head you probably felt the need to protect me, even if it meant you suffered."

"Yes, I felt the need to protect you. To protect you from the horrifying events I saw that night. I promised him I'd look after you and keep you safe and knowing that I did a shitty job of that makes me fucking sick inside."

"You didn't."

"I did, Bailey. I blew it with you. I didn't do as I promised."

"You are wrong. The only way you blew it was by not talking to me. You don't deserve to suffer alone." She pulled the sweatshirt down off the hook and turned to look at me. "You want things to be back to the way they were? You need to share with me how you feel. Stop worrying about me, stop trying to protect me, and let me help you carry whatever it is you are feeling and dealing with."

She studied my eyes and stood there waiting with tears

running down her face for me to answer her, but I couldn't. I couldn't burden her with my guilt. So instead of opening up to her, I shook my head. "I can't."

"You can't or you won't? There is a difference," she demanded, standing there with her hand on her hip. "Look, what happened, happened to both of us, Jackson."

"No, it didn't. You lost a brother."

"So did you. All I ever wanted from you was for you to open up and share with me how you felt. I wanted you to share what you were going through, but you pretended to be okay when you were with me when, in fact, you were blaming yourself inside. Sure, I didn't make it any better, and I know that, but I felt very jilted when you couldn't talk to me but you'd go sit and talk to some therapist, a stranger, in a cold office."

I looked at her. I could tell she wasn't just saying that, but I still couldn't shake the feeling of blame I felt either. "I know that was all you wanted," I whispered, still not fully prepared to share with her the memories of the dreams that had been haunting me all this time.

"Then talk to me," she pleaded as she walked up to me and wrapped her arms around me, resting her head on my chest. I placed my arms around her, holding her close to me. "I miss him, Jackson," she murmured, her face pressed into my shirt. "I miss him so much."

I pulled her tighter against me and closed my eyes as I

rested my chin on the top of her head. "Me too," I whispered, kissing the top of her head. "So much."

"Were you dreaming of him?"

I closed my eyes and was silent; the dreams haunting my thoughts again. No matter how badly I wanted to tell her, those dreams paralyzed me. I couldn't open up to her. She didn't press me. Instead, she gave me a few minutes and when I didn't answer her she slipped out from my grasp. She didn't look back, she pulled the door open and walked out the front door without looking back at me, just as she had five years ago.

# Bailey

I was so happy that the lunch rush was over. I cleared and washed the last few tables a few minutes ago and now stood behind the counter finishing stacking the clean glasses behind the bar. It had been busier than normal, and we had a bit of time to get the place ready for dinner and the rest of the night. I had just finished washing down the bar when the door opened. I looked up to see Cara walk in, waving at me as she climbed up on a stool.

"Hey, what brings you here?" I asked, smiling.

"I got off work early and saw your car out front and thought I would pop in and see you. I didn't think you were working until later tonight."

"I wasn't supposed to. One girl called in sick, and since I called in yesterday, I figured I'd take the shift. I could use the money."

"How are you doing?" Cara asked, giving me a concerned look.

I shrugged. It had been five years since my brother's death, and this was the first year since that I had been back in Sunset Cove. How did she think I was? "All right, I guess."

"Are you guys going to the police memorial dinner tomorrow?"

"I don't know. Mom wants me to take her."

"You should go."

"I know I should. I just don't know if I'm feeling up to it. Did you want something to drink?"

"I'll have a soda." Cara smiled, shrugged her coat off, and placed it on a stool beside her.

I quickly poured her a glass and placed it down in front of her. She took a sip of her drink and smiled at me. "You see, Jackson lately?"

"Seriously?" I questioned, turning my back toward her, continuing to place the glasses from the dishwasher to the bar.

"What?"

"Did you come here to see me, or talk about him?" I sounded annoyed. I knew I did, but this was exactly the stress I'd been talking about when I told him I wasn't ready to get involved again. I also knew that had Cara and Ryan not been gone away for the last couple of weeks, she'd of been all over me about him.

"I came here to see you. I just figured you guys looked chummy the morning of the brunch... and perhaps... I don't know... a spark lit."

I had zero right to bite her head off the way I had. "Sorry."

"It's okay. I will take that as a yes, then."

I turned and rolled my eyes at her. "Seriously, just ask me what you want to know."

"Are you guys back together? Amanda was sure she saw you two at the movies the other night," she questioned, leaning forward on the bar. Exactly the Cara I knew. She wasted no time in asking me what she wanted to know.

"We have spent time together, yes."

"Is it serious?"

I closed my eyes and tried to figure out what to say. Was it serious? I wanted to say yes. I wanted to say we were back together, but after what had happened the other night, I wasn't sure. We hadn't spoken since. I fished through my mind, trying to determine what I was okay telling her. I didn't want her to know about the night of the wedding or the morning of the brunch.

"Bailey?"

"I don't know," I said in a low voice. "Why?"

"No reason."

"Cara?" I knew she knew something, and I would not allow her to come in here and ask me all these questions

215

without giving me the courtesy of telling me what she knew.

"He stopped in at the house last night. He helped Ryan work on the car."

"That's nice, but I don't understand what him dropping by your house has to do with how serious we are?" I said, turning to finish putting glasses up on the shelves.

"Bailey, I went out to drop off a couple of beers, and I heard them talking. They were under the car and did not know I was even there. They were talking about you. He told Ryan that he loves you, and he said that you guys were together the other night, and that you ran off. He's concerned about you."

I was so glad that I wasn't facing her at that given moment. I could feel my eyes burning at her words, and I closed them tight to stop the tears from falling. I knew he loved me. There wasn't a doubt in my mind. I knew he loved me, and always would. He never stopped loving me, even on the day I walked out on him, and I knew deep down inside that I loved him, too.

"I know," I answered weakly and swallowed hard, trying to clear the large lump that sat in my throat. There was no use keeping it a secret any longer. "I love him too," I said, turning and looking over at my friend, tears filling my eyes. It was the first time I'd admitted I still had feelings for him to another person in a long time.

"Oh, Bailey, what happened?"

I took a deep breath, not sure if I was ready to talk about it. Yet I knew I needed to, no matter how much it hurt. I wiped my eyes. "It was the same thing that happened when I left the first time. He still won't talk to me, Cara."

"He won't talk to you?"

"About Connor."

"So, Ryan barely talks to me about work things. That's what he uses the others for. Don't be so hard on him. There are just things that we don't need to know."

"Hard on him. Please, I was nothing more than patient. Do you know he still has those nightmares?"

"How do you know that?"

"Because I spent the other night at his place, and I woke up to arms flailing and him talking in his sleep, sweating up a storm. Do you have any clue how it makes me feel when I ask him about it, and he just says it's nothing, and not to worry about it? We both suffered a loss. I just don't think it's fair that he feels I should talk to him, but he won't talk to me. That is just a double-edged sword. What am I supposed to do?"

Cara looked at me, sadness in her eyes. I knew she had the best intentions coming here, but she was opening a territory she knew very little about. Jackson and I had kept most of this part of our troubles secret. I knew she was aware of exactly why we parted ways, but neither of us had truly shared everything openly with our friends. She was about to say something when the door opened and three couples walked in, followed by another two. I had never been happier to see people than I was at that moment. This was a conversation I couldn't have right now.

"I'll be right back." I said, signaling to the empty tables while grabbing a pile of menus.

The dinner rush went off with little excitement, and I was so happy to see Carly, instead of Marcus, walk in at eight. Tonight was the pool league, and we knew it would be busy. Glenn was in the back, I was at the bar, and Carly was delivering drinks to tables when the door opened and in walked the same three guys from the Green Cobras. The same three who had caused all the trouble a few months ago.

Immediately, I walked to the back and pulled Glenn out front, leaving Marcus to stock the cooler alone.

"Glenn, those guys are back." I wasn't in the mood to deal with trouble tonight as I glanced over my shoulder to see the one watching me.

"Why don't you head on your last break, and I will watch the bar," Glenn said, taking over at the drink station.

I nodded. "Thanks." I grabbed a container of fries and a soda from the kitchen and headed out the side door to the back alley. The cold winter air felt good against my warm skin, and I parked myself on the metal stairs of the fire escape. I sat there eating the hot fries and sipping on the soda, while sending texts to Cara, when I heard a low whistle come from behind me. A chill ran through me as I turned around to look over my shoulder.

"What do we have here?" I recognized Garrick immediately as his eyes locked on me. He slowly walked toward me, taking me in.

I could feel the panic rising in my chest as he came closer, but I did my best to keep a level head. I looked him over, taking in the colors on the patch of his jacket, to the chain that went from his belt loop to his wallet.

"Nothing. We have nothing here."

"Doesn't look like nothing to me." His eyes ran the length of my body, giving me the creeps. "You're a pretty little thing, you know that. You were here the other night, weren't you? I'd certainly like to get to know you a lot better."

I stood up and backed up, putting a little space between us, and slowly made my way back toward the side door. I was just about to pull the door open when his hand gripped my arm. He spun me around, causing me to drop my food and drink and there, pressed against the wall, he placed one hand on each side of my body. I could smell the booze pouring off his breath as he leaned into me.

"What's your name?" he hissed into my ear. He was close enough to me I could feel his breath against my skin.

I could barely breathe as he ran his rough ringed fingers down my cheek.

"Bailey," I cried, paralyzed with fear. As his eyes locked with mine, I realized I hadn't mentioned to anyone that I was coming out back for my break, which meant no one knew I was out here. I could taste the bile in the back of my throat as panic filled me.

"You got a boyfriend?" he questioned, his lips practically touching my ear as he whispered the words. I felt his fingers run across my bare skin, between my shirt and the waist of my jeans.

I closed my eyes tightly; every nerve in my body was on high alert as he continued touching me. "Yes," I whimpered.

"Oh yeah? What's his name?" His fingers continued dancing across my bare skin.

"Jackson," I whimpered.

"Jackson, huh?"

"Yeah," I said, doing my best to keep my voice strong. It was no use. I knew I was failing at that.

"Hmmm, you know what? I think you are lying to me."

I closed my eyes as his thumb grazed the underside of my breast.

"Get away from her, Garrick.," I heard a familiar deep voice say.

"Hey, buddy, why don't you just fuck off?"

I kept my eyes closed. I was immobilized, filled with fear. I did not know who was in the alley with us or where they had come from, but I prayed it took this guy's concentration from me. However, when I felt his finger trail down my cheek again, I figured the guy had probably taken off, leaving me to fend for myself.

"I will not tell you again, Garrick, get away from her." I peered from one eye and saw Jackson, in his uniform, standing in the doorway.

"Jackson," I cried.

"Bailey, get inside. He will not hurt you," he demanded.

Garrick let out a low chuckle. "This is your boyfriend." Garrick scoffed. "I could wipe the floor with him." He said, running his thumb once again across the underside of my breast.

The taste of bile was stronger now, and my throat burned as I swallowed.

"Bailey, now," Jackson barked.

I didn't waste any time. I darted from the fence Garrick had created with his arms and pushed by Jackson, slipping in through the back door. Leaning up against the wall, I took a few deep breaths while listening to what was going on in the alley.

"Garrick, you guys have been causing enough trouble in here lately. I suggest you all find a different place to hang out."

"Fuck off, Walker, or I'll come after you next."

I couldn't move. It alarmed me at the fact that he knew Jackson's last name when only a few moments ago he pretended not to even know him.

"That sounds like a threat, Garrick. Are you threatening me?"

"Nope."

"I didn't think so. Take yourself and get out of here now. Specter won't be happy to know you are around these parts again."

"Perhaps I'll solve that problem, just like I did with the last one who said that to me," Garrick gritted.

Alarm bells ran through me at his threat. I strained to hear, but just after the words had passed his lips, the outside door was pushed shut, and I could no longer hear what was going on. Panic filled me as the seconds turned to minutes. Finally, the door opened, and Jackson stepped inside, closing the door behind him, and my eyes filled with tears at the sight of him.

I closed my eyes and forced myself to think of anything but what had just happened. It was the only chance I had to keep the sobs from escaping. I felt his hands on me. I'd know his touch anywhere. "Are you all right?" he questioned as I leaned against the wall and covered my mouth to keep from seeing the food I'd eaten come back in reverse. I nodded my head and closed my eyes.

"I am now," I answered, wrapping my arms around him. The comfort from his touch soothed me and I took a deep breath, blinking away my tears. "What are you doing here?"

"Glenn called. A fight broke out inside, then he realized you were missing. Are you sure you're okay? He didn't put his hands on you, did he? Other than what I saw," Jackson questioned, gripping me by the arms and looking me over. "I swear to god, I'll fucking kill him if he did." He bit out, his jaw tight.

I shook my head. "No, he didn't. Just scared me. How does he know your name?" I questioned, meeting Jackson's eyes.

"Small town troublemakers, Bailey. These guys deal with most of us on a weekly basis," he said, pulling me against him for a hug.

"You sure that is all it is? Like, he's not going to come after you, is he?"

"No, he won't." He answered, glancing down the hall toward the entrance to the bar. "What time are you finished?"

"I close tonight."

Jackson met my eyes. I could tell from the look on his face he wanted to protect me. I knew that meant he wanted me to come to his place tonight, so he knew where I was and that I was safe in his arms. I wanted that too, but was too afraid to say that to him.

"Be careful driving home, okay? Don't walk to your car alone."

"I will. I mean, I will be careful driving home and I won't walk to my car alone." I answered, taking in the sadness in his eyes.

Instead of leaning forward and kissing me, he turned and left me standing alone in the back room. I wanted to call him, tell him to come back, but I just stood and watched as he walked away from me.

# Jackson

"Not eating?" Asher asked, sitting down across from me and placing a cold bottle of water in front of me. "You should eat."

I looked over at Ryan and Dave, who were manning the barbeque, and shook my head. "No, I'm not hungry."

I looked through the crowd, scanning the scene for the one person I still hadn't seen today. I'd hoped she'd have been here. I wanted to have a minute with her, to talk to her, especially now that some time had passed. But the more time passed, the more I was convinced that she wouldn't be coming.

"So how's things with Bailey?" Asher asked, taking a bite of the burger that sat in front of him. "I saw she spent the night."

"How the hell you know that?"

"I saw her car in your driveway. I was going to come and knock on the door but figured you might just kick my ass, especially if you were...you know." Asher spread his fingers and brought them to his mouth, sticking his tongue between them, a shit-eating grin on his face.

"Well, at least you were smart enough not to find out." I chuckled.

"So, how are things with her?"

"Same as always," I bit out, wishing I could give him a different answer.

"Here, I hoped that the two of you might be back together."

I ignored the comment and looked through the crowd one more time. It was then that I finally saw her standing beside her mother. They were engaged in a conversation with the two officers who oversaw Connor's case.

"Have you told her about the dreams?" Asher asked, pulling me back to our conversation.

"What is it with you and the million questions today?" I barked as I watched Bailey leave her mother's side and cross the park over to the water's edge, where she sat down on the grass and looked out over the water. The confrontation I'd had with Garrick the other night still tormented me. The words he had spewed at me once I had shut the door to the alley ate at me. Connor had been actively investigating the Green Cobras when he'd been killed, and the threats Garrick had thrown at me had me wondering if he perhaps Connor hadn't been onto him. I wondered if he wasn't the one responsible for Connor.

"What's with you, Walker?" Dave questioned, sitting down with a plate full of food, Ryan following.

I knew this wasn't the time or the place to bring this up, but I didn't feel it could wait. "Dave, after Connor died, did you guys investigate any of the Cobra members as suspects? I mean, he was actively investigating them when shit went down. It is a possibility that he ran into one of them."

Asher, Ryan, and Dave all stopped chewing their food and looked up at me. "I don't think this is the time to talk about this, Jackson," Dave bit out and nodded to the people who were surrounding us.

He was right, and I knew it. The incident had incited a lot of unrest for every citizen of Sunset Cove. It was the first time in over twenty-five years one of our members had been killed in the line of duty. Those things just didn't happen here.

I ignored his warning and lowered my voice. "Dave, seriously, it's been five years, and we have no more leads than we did that night. I think it's time that we look at them, especially one of them—Garrick Barton. We know for a fact that those men were in the area that night. I just had a run-in with him the other night, and he said some things to me that lead me to believe he might..."

"So, they were in the area. Connor was alone. You saw

a shadow of a man who resembled his height and build but no face. That's it. There was nothing on the video feeds from the alley, and no other witnesses. We can't just go making suspects up out of suspicion."

"Dammit, Dave, please, just listen to me," I said, smashing my fist on the table, which pulled a lot of attention over to the four of us.

"Jackson, it's enough," Dave bit out, giving me a look of warning.

I stared back at Dave, searching his eyes for any more allowance of what we had been talking about, but I saw none. Instead, he went back to eating, talking to Asher and Ryan while I sat there waiting for the tension between the four of us to dissipate. Ryan soon had them all laughing, and soon it was as if none of the talk between us had even happened.

"Hey, Bailey," Asher said, looking behind me as the others greeted her, and I turned in time to see Bailey approaching us.

"Hey, guys," she said, smiling.

I stood up, and she surprised me by immediately wrapping her arms around me, pressing her body up against mine.

"Everything okay?" I whispered in her ear.

"Yeah. I just thought I would come over and say hi. I wanted to let you know I'm going to take Mom home now. She says she is tired. I'm tired myself, and I have to work tonight," she said, looking up at me, her eyes hiding something.

"Okay," I said, pushing a strand of hair from her face. "Everything else, okay?"

She shrugged and looked at Asher, Ryan, and Dave. "Do you have a minute?"

I nodded and turned to the guys. "I'll be right back. Let Mike know I will be back in time to man the grill."

"Nice to see you, Bailey." Dave waved.

"You too, Dave."

As we walked away, I heard Ryan invite Bailey's mom to sit down with them and offer her a burger. "She's in excellent hands." I said, my voice low.

"I know." She said, slipping her hand into mine. We finally found a quiet spot over in the corner of the room.

"What's up?" I asked, looking into her eyes to see them lined with worry.

"Um, I am not sure how to tell you this," she bit out, almost on the verge of tears.

"Tell me what?"

When she wouldn't look at me, I placed my hand on the side of her cheek and turned her head toward me.

"I was sitting outside. I needed to get some air and that Garrick guy approached me again."

I felt every muscle in my body tighten. "What? Did he put his hands on you?"

"No." She sniffled. "I ignored him, told him to go

away, but he wouldn't. Instead, he kneeled beside me and started asking me questions about you and I."

"What questions?"

Her cheeks were red, and she avoided my eyes.

"What questions, Bailey?"

"Questions about…" She swallowed hard. "About our personal life."

"About sex?" I asked through clenched teeth.

She slowly nodded her head. "He wanted to know if you…"

Anger shot through me while I waited for her.

"If you pleasure me."

"You're sure he didn't touch you?" I barked, pulling her against me.

She nodded. "He didn't. I refused to answer him, and I got up and came inside to see my mom, but he stopped me. He told me he would see me tonight at work. That he would wait at the end of the bar like you do because you wouldn't be able to be there. Then he took off."

Bailey put her face in her hands and sobbed. I pulled her against me while I scanned the room for signs of him or any other member of the Green Cobras, but saw nothing out of place.

"You don't need to worry. I will be in the bar later tonight, okay? I will make sure I am there to pick you up." I whispered, placing my thumb and finger under her chin, tilting her head back, leaning in and meeting her lips.

"Until that time, I'll have one of the other guys come and watch."

"Jackson, you don't have to do that. He just gives me the creeps, I guess," she said, wrapping her arms around me, giving me a hug. "Please be careful tonight," she whispered in my ear.

"Always am, you know that."

She kissed me once more before heading off toward her mother, while I stood there still scanning the venue for Garrick. If I found him here, I knew I'd kill him.

# Bailey

I'd gone home after the memorial and slept for a few hours before going in for my shift. From the time I'd run into Garrick, spoke to Jackson, and had left the memorial to now, I'd had a funny feeling that something bad was going to happen. I did my best to put that silly thought to the back of my mind and push on with my night.

The bar was packed, and I could barely hear Cara over the music in the bar. "What did you say?" I shouted as I turned the music down a little.

"I asked if you were doing okay?" she shouted over the bar and then let out a laugh.

The music had been cranked all night, people were everywhere, and I had never been more thankful for being on bar duty. It saved me having to make my way through the crowd time and time again, taking orders and then going back out to find people. I glanced over at the clock and signaled to Glenn that it was just about closing time. Glenn flipped the music off, not bothering to offer a last call. I gathered up the mess of bottles and caps on the bar counter. I was looking forward to having the place to ourselves. It took a little longer than thirty minutes for the bar to empty, and once the bouncers escorted the last patrons outside, I walked over to the door and turned the lock. My stomach turning at the fact that I still hadn't seen Jackson tonight.

"You sure you're all right?" Cara asked as I walked back in behind the bar.

"Yeah, just worried about Jackson," I said as I started collecting glasses from a nearby table. "He promised me he would stop by after work because of what happened today."

"Don't worry. I heard from Ryan a couple of hours ago. They were swamped tonight. The calls never stopped. I mean, just look at this place. I'm shocked you guys didn't have to call them tonight."

"True. Look, I just need to run in the back to get some cleaner. I'll turn the TV on for you, okay?"

"Thanks, babe. Can I get a soda before you go?"

I quickly grabbed a glass and poured Cara a soda, and then made my way into the back to grab some cleaner.

Once I had filled my bottle, I grabbed three plates of left-over fries from the kitchen and took them out front, dropping them down in front of Cara and Glenn. Then I took a tray and started collecting more glasses from the floor. The place was a mess, and I already knew it was going to take me a while to get it cleaned up. I had just picked up my tray full of dirty glasses when I heard Cara gasp.

"Bailey, quick, can you turn up the TV?" she asked, standing up from the stool she was sitting on.

I walked fast, placing my tray on the bar. "What is it?" I questioned as I reached for the remote when I caught the headline on the TV. I turned up the volume and stood watching the nightmare unfold before my eyes.

"They have released no names. Again, a robbery in progress turned bad. Two Sunset Cove officers are dead, and they have transported one other to the hospital, injuries unknown. Suspect is still at large," the news reporter stated.

The room spun and my vision blurred as I stared up at the screen; the words blurring together, and then the room went black.

"Bailey. Bailey. Please wake up."

I blinked, slowly opening my eyes. It surprised me to find Glenn sitting beside me, his arm around me. Cara sat across from me, a look of worry on her face, and then Marcus appeared with a glass of water.

"What...what happened?" I asked, looking at them both.

"You fainted. After you heard the news."

I looked at both Cara and Glenn, unsure of what they were talking about. "The news?"

"The shooting," Cara bit out, Glenn giving her a look. "I've been trying to get hold of Ryan, but he hasn't answered yet."

"What about Jackson?"

Cara looked to Glenn and then back to me. "He's not answering either." She said, her voice low.

"We need to get to the hospital," I said, trying to get up, but Glenn wouldn't allow me to.

"Bailey, you just fainted. I think you need to wait a little longer. Make sure you are all right before you get up."

"Yeah, I agree. I'm monitoring my phone, Bailey," Cara said, rubbing my thigh.

"No, we need to go. Please, I'll get my stuff," I said as Glenn helped me slowly sit up, then helping me stand, making sure I was steady on my feet before I took a step.

My heart was in my throat as we walked into the entrance of the hospital. Immediately, Cara went over to the information desk and, in a panic, started asking if they had any information on the officer who had been shot. I watched as the woman behind the desk shook her head, refusing to give her any information. I hung my head and looked around when I finally spotted Dave Specter standing off in the corner, talking on his cell phone.

I walked over and tapped Cara on the shoulder, but she shrugged me off and continued bombarding the nurse with questions.

"Come, Cara, I know where they are," I said, pulling on her arm, smiling at the girl behind the desk who looked annoyed.

"What? Where are they?" she said, almost falling as she stumbled over the carpet.

"Dave is right there," I said, pointing in his direction.

We both walked over and stood in front of Dave. Every part of my body remembered this exact scene. It had happened only a few short years ago. My eyes burned at the memory of the night Connor had been killed. It was like I was stuck reliving that night all over again. Everything, right down to the smell, was the same.

"Any news?" Cara questioned as Dave looked at both of us.

"Ryan is fine, Cara. He just went to grab some coffees," Dave said, looking at me with a look I had seen once before. Panic filled my body, and everything seemed to move to a dream-like state as I stood there looking back at Dave.

"Oh thank God," Cara said, sitting down on the closest chair, looking relieved.

I couldn't even focus on Cara or anything she had said as I looked back at Dave, waiting for the news I already knew I wasn't ready to hear. He went to say something, but I held my hand up, stopping him. I tried to take a deep breath as a feeling of dread filled me. My chest felt like it was going to explode at any minute, and I covered my mouth to stop the sobs from escaping.

Dave took hold of me by the shoulders and walked me over to a quiet corner where we had a little privacy, yet not far away from Cara. "It's Jackson, sweetie. He's in surgery. We are waiting to hear."

In that instant, every ounce of air had been sucked from the room, and I turned around to gather whatever strength I had in me. Instead of strength, all I felt was myself crumbling with each second that passed. I was numb all over, and I turned back to see Dave standing there looking at me. I felt his hands on my shoulders and immediately I collapsed into him, hugging him tight as I allowed the tears to fall.

"He has to be okay, right?" I cried. "I mean, he has to be."

Dave said nothing. He just hugged me tight as I sobbed, mumbling those same words repeatedly.

"Come, Bailey, sit down." Dave guided me over to the empty chair beside Cara and helped me sit down. "Cara, can you please get a tea for Bailey?"

"Of course."

Before I knew it, Dave held a hot cup of tea out for me to take. "Just sip on this, okay?" he said, sitting on the edge of a chair beside me.

I took a sip of the hot liquid and tried to calm myself down. I looked at Cara, who placed her hand on my thigh.

"Sir, can we speak to you for a moment?"

I looked up to see two young uniformed officers standing before us, waiting to talk to Dave. Dave made sure I was okay before getting up and moving off to the side with the other two officers. Cara and Ryan now sat with me, doing their best to distract me, when Dave approached us.

"I've got to head back to the station. They've brought in the guys we've been looking for," he said, clearing his throat.

"The guy responsible for doing this to Jackson?" I asked.

Dave nodded. "A member of the Green Cobras, Dorian Patton," he said and turned to leave the hospital.

My blood ran cold at the name of the Green Cobras

member. I got up and ran after Dave, finally getting his attention just outside of the emergency room doors.

"Bailey, what is it?" he questioned.

"Dave, I just wanted to let you know that Garrick and Jackson had a confrontation the other night at The Crooked Judge. I didn't hear what they said, but I am sure he threatened Jackson. Garrick also approached me in the park today at the picnic. He wanted to know things about Jackson and I." I said, my voice low, my cheeks heating. "He's been after me since the first night he walked into The Crooked Judge. Anyway, he said something about meeting me at the bar tonight and waiting to take me home since my boyfriend wouldn't be able to."

"Thanks for letting me know," he said. "Now you get inside, rest."

I thanked Dave and watched him walk across the dark parking lot of the hospital before returning to the waiting room to wait with Cara and Ryan. The next three hours felt like forever. We all sat there quietly, watching the same news reel replay. I was going to ask Ryan to ask a hospital staff to turn the channel off when my stomach spun. Only I didn't have to because, finally, a doctor appeared in the waiting doorway.

"Who's here with Jackson Walker?" he asked.

"We are," Ryan called, holding his hand up in the air.

The doctor walked over to us and smiled. "Hi. I'm Doctor Maddox. The surgery went fine. He was lucky. We were able to remove all bullets and fragments. It took a little longer than we expected, but there were no complications."

"Can we see him?" I asked, sitting forward, ready to jump up if he said yes.

"I'm afraid not. He's still in recovery for another hour. As soon as they move him up to his room, then we can allow one person in. So whoever is related," he said, looking at all three of us.

"That would be me," I said, standing up.

# Jackson

The steady sound of beeping woke me. As my eyes adjusted, I looked around at the unfamiliar surroundings. My name was written on a whiteboard that hung on the wall at the foot of my bed. I looked around. An IV pole hung on the bedside, and then I spotted the machine that was responsible for the monotonous beeping sound. Why was I in the hospital? How had I gotten here? I shifted in the bed and went to roll over but stopped when I felt a sharp pain followed by a pull in my side.

"Oh, God," I cried, gripping my side. I lifted the blanket and looked down at a large white bandage that covered my side. I took a deep breath and looked to my right, where all the machines sat, monitoring one thing or another. Then I looked over to my left and that was when I saw Bailey. She was curled up in a chair, sound asleep.

Her jacket was rolled up under her neck like a makeshift pillow, and a blanket was over her lap.

I lay back and blew out a breath, trying hard to get comfortable. It took time, but I finally found a position that was comfortable enough that I could relax back against the pillows. The door to my room opened, and a nurse walked in. She was quiet and smiled as she came over to a machine and hit a few buttons, printing a report. Then she replaced an IV bag. "Good morning," she whispered. "It's nice to see you are finally awake."

"What am I doing here?" I questioned, looking at the machine she was fiddling with.

"You were shot. You had surgery," she said, reconnecting the tubes to the IV and taking my vitals.

"How long has she been here?" I asked, looking over at Bailey, who was still sound asleep.

"She spent the night. She was very concerned and refused to leave, so I got her the chair and the blanket."

"She was concerned?" I asked. I could hear the surprise in my voice at her admission.

"Yes, very. I sat with her for a while last night after she came up. She was extremely upset. We talked for a while. I took her mind off of things. At least I think I did. You know, you're a lucky man. You have a very special girl there."

I looked over and just took her in. She was so beautiful, and I thanked God that she was here with me. She was my everything. I just wished I had realized it sooner than I did because I feared it took me too long.

"I know," I whispered.

The nurse smiled. "Get some more rest. The doctor will be in after breakfast. Did you need anything?"

"Maybe a little water?"

"Sure thing."

Once she returned with a cool glass of water, I had a few sips and then relaxed back against the pillow and closed my eyes. The pain in my side was a little unbearable, but instead of focusing on that, I looked over to Bailey. I'd been watching her for a while when she finally opened her eyes, looking confused, and then a look of joy came over her face.

"You're awake. Thank God," Bailey said, throwing the covers off her lap and getting up, coming over to my side. She gently sat down on the edge of the bed, careful not to move it too much.

I grabbed hold of her hand and smiled.

"How are you feeling?" she asked, gripping my hand tight in hers.

"Okay, a little sore." I groaned, gripping my side. "Okay, wait, a lot sore. What happened?"

"You were shot. I don't know much more than that. Ryan and Dave said they'd be by later today."

I looked at Bailey as a look of concern washed over her face. I'd seen that look before, the same look that she had when she walked out on me five years earlier. I felt the panic rise in my chest as she now avoided my eyes.

"What is it?" I asked.

"Nothing. I was so scared. I thought I would never see you again." She looked up at me, eyes full of tears.

"Bailey, no tears. It's okay. I'm all right."

Bailey's eyes were full of tears. I carefully shifted myself over and tapped the mattress beside me. She didn't hesitate. She climbed up onto the bed and carefully curled into the opposite side of my injury and rested her head on my shoulder. I wrapped my arm around her and pressed a kiss to her forehead, trying to calm her.

"I'm okay." I whispered.

She let out a sob. "I know. I was just so afraid I was going to lose you." She sniffled.

"You just stay there. I'll come around and help you," Bailey said as she climbed out of the car and ran around to the passenger's side to help me out.

Even though I was perfectly capable of getting out of the car alone, I waited for her to come around and open the door. With my bag slung over her shoulder, she helped me to the front door and waited while I slipped my key in the lock.

When I stepped inside, it surprised me to see Cara, Ryan, Dave, and a bunch of other guys from the station standing in my living room.

"Welcome home," Cara said, stepping forward and wrapping her arms around me.

"Thanks. It's good to finally be out of there. Thought I was going to have to make a jailbreak." I chuckled as I shook hands with a few of my fellow officers.

Bailey was oddly quiet, and even though she was polite with everyone, I knew something was bothering her, and I was sure I knew exactly what that something was. She smiled and then placed her hand on my shoulder. "I'm just going to take this bag down to your room, then I'm going to start some of your laundry while I'm here." She whispered in my ear.

"You're not going to stay here with everyone?" I questioned, looking into her eyes. I wanted her here with me, with our friends and family. It about broke my heart when she shook her head and dropped her eyes from mine.

Instead, she turned, and I noticed she and Cara made eye contact. Then she turned back to me, softly smiled, and placed a kiss on my cheek. "You just enjoy yourself, okay?" she whispered, placing another kiss on my cheek before turning and leaving. Everyone was quiet, and they looked my way with concern as she slipped down the hall. It was only a matter of moments before the talking started again and soon the room was filled with laughter, while we all shared stories and relived some of our greater takedowns.

As the afternoon passed, officers came and went. It was great seeing everyone, but soon it was just Ryan, Cara, Dave, and I. Bailey hadn't made an appearance all afternoon. Instead, she claimed she wanted to make sure that everything was clean and organized for me.

She'd just brought in a plate of food and made a little small talk with Ryan before returning to the kitchen without so much as a glance in my direction.

Cara leaned over, a look of concern on her face, and whispered, "Is she okay?"

"I don't know. She's been funny for the last week. It's like she has something she wants to say but won't."

"I'll talk to her," Cara said, standing, taking some plates into the kitchen.

As soon as she was gone, Dave cleared his throat and leaned in closer to me. "Jackson, I wanted to let you know we arrested Dorian Patton the night of your shooting. He turned Garrick in to us, gave us everything. We just need to find him, but in the meantime, we had forensics examine the bullet casings that we found at the scene against the one we found at the scene the night Connor was shot."

I almost didn't believe what I was hearing. "Don't leave me in suspense. What did you find out?"

"It matched. It was the same one Connor was shot with," he said, keeping his voice low. "You were right. It was Garrick. I'm sorry I didn't want to hear about it."

"Have you told Bailey?" I could feel excitement building at the fact that we had finally found his killer.

"Not yet. It's not a matter of public record yet. We are launching a full investigation into this guy, but as of right now, there is a warrant out for his arrest. He is up for charges in relation to both incidents."

"Good to know. Thanks."

"On that note, I must get going. Got to get back to the station. Jackson, I'm glad you are home. Enjoy your time off. Ryan, don't be late for your shift, or so help me." Dave chuckled as he made his way out the front door.

As Dave pulled the door shut, Cara and Bailey stepped into the living room. Bailey looked around at the mess of plates and glasses and then met my eyes.

"Bailey, did you want some help to clean this mess up?" Cara questioned.

"You don't have to. I'll be fine." She shrugged.

"No, come on. I'm not leaving you with all this mess," Cara said, getting up and stacking dishes into a pile. "You guys just relax."

Bailey wouldn't hear of it, and instantly began helping Cara clear up all the dishes and put everything away. Once finished, Ryan and Cara said their goodbyes and started home. The second the door had closed on their car, Bailey started gathering her things and turned to look my way.

"I think I'm going to head home."

"Why? I was hoping you'd stay, maybe watch a movie with me. Perhaps help me to bed." I winked, tugging on the bottom of her t-shirt.

I watched her look around the room, as if she was looking for a reason or excuse why she couldn't stay.

"Come on, sit down," I said, flipping the TV on and patting the empty spot beside me on the couch.

With hesitation, she hung up her sweater and keys. "Did you want anything from the kitchen?"

I shook my head. "Nope, I just want you."

She wandered over and sat down beside me. I lay down and put my head in her lap, then flipped the channels until I found a movie for us to watch. We were about halfway through the movie when I looked up and noticed that Bailey wasn't really watching the movie. Instead, she just sat there staring out the front window, a faraway look in her eyes.

"Are you okay?" I questioned. "You've been quiet all afternoon."

She looked down at me as her eyes welled with tears. "Jackson, I—I can't do this."

"You can't do what?"

"This. I can't do this. I can't do us. I can't be with you

and be so afraid that every time you walk out that door, you won't come back. I can't take it. You almost didn't come home, and it was at that moment I realized just how much I love you. I can't lose you too."

"Babe, I'll always come home. You don't need to worry about that."

Tears now streamed down her cheeks. "Those were the same words my brother always told us and look what happened. Look what just happened. You could have died on that table in that hospital... You could have..." Sobs wracked her body as she buried her face into her hands.

I carefully sat up and was about to wrap my arms around her when she got up from the couch. She grabbed her purse and coat and turned to look at me, her eyes red and watery.

"I'm sorry. I just can't do this with you again. I've got to go."

I didn't have time to say anything before she bolted out the front door and went down the steps. There was no way I could chase after her. I couldn't move that fast, so instead I watched from the window as she got into her car and peeled out of my driveway.

# Bailey

The dark-gray sky matched my mood perfectly this morning. I took a hot shower, dried my hair, and got dressed, then made my way to the kitchen for a quick cup of coffee before going to meet Mom. I was still hunting for a place just on the outskirts of Sunset Cove. I couldn't stay here. There were just too many memories that still haunted me, and one man I knew I would never get over if I ran into him all the time.

After Jackson had returned home from the hospital and I ran out on him, I vowed not to return to see him. I'd come home in a panic and let Mom know that, as soon as I could arrange it, I would be leaving. Mom had cried herself to sleep that night. I heard the sobs coming from her bedroom. I felt awful and I too lay in bed that night with tears streaming down my face. In the morning, she made me promise her I wouldn't move too far away this time, and she'd asked that I stay at least for Christmas. She also made me promise to have dinner with her every Sunday, either at my place or at hers. When I looked at my mother's sad, bloodshot eyes, I couldn't refuse. Later that afternoon, she had asked me to accompany her to the cemetery to place a Christmas wreath on Connor's grave. I couldn't refuse to do that either.

I pulled my car up alongside the cemetery and cut the engine. This was the first time since the day we buried my brother that I had returned to this spot. I leaned back against the seat, trying to calm the feeling in the pit of my stomach.

I took my time walking through the snow over to where my brother's gravesite was. I could already see Mom in the distance saying a prayer. I hung my head and continued my slow walk, finally coming up behind her. I stood there quietly, listening to her hum one of her favorite songs. She removed the fall wreath, wiped away the marks on the tombstone before placing the winter one.

"Those were his favorite colors," I said, looking down at the mix of red and white flowers on the Christmas wreath.

"Yes, I know, and Christmas was his favorite time of year. I neglected bringing a Christmas wreath here long enough, so I figured today was as good a day as any," she said, placing the fall wreath down in the snow. Once she'd finished, she stood back and looked down at it.

"How is Jackson doing?" She questioned quietly.

I shrugged. "Okay, I guess."

"Bailey, you mean to tell me you really haven't spoken to him? Goodness, they shot the man. He may need help with things around the house."

I shook my head, fighting back the tears that threatened to fall. I was feeling overly emotional today and really didn't want to talk about Jackson. In fact, I just wanted this time of year to be over with.

"He'll be okay. Ryan and Cara have been checking in on him. He's in great hands."

Mom stood up and brushed the snow off the knees of her pants, then looked at me. "Bailey, I always promised never to get involved in your private life. But there comes a time when a mother tires of watching her daughter make the same mistakes repeatedly."

I frowned. "What's that supposed to mean?" I asked defensively.

"It means that you're being a stubborn fool. You love the man. I know you have been seeing him."

"No, I haven't."

"Bailey, I'm not stupid. I know you snuck off with him the night of the wedding, and I know you have been sneaking around with him ever since. All those times you claimed you were with Cara, I know the actual truth. You were with Jackson."

I looked at the small smile that rested on my mother's lips. "How did you know that?"

"Bailey, do you think because you moved away that I don't know you? You are wrong because I know you well. I'm your mother. I know you better than you know yourself, my dear."

I shook my head in denial. "Mom, please. Don't get involved."

"Do you honestly think I don't know the things you've done? I know it all. I know about the times Jackson climbed in your window when you were only fifteen. I also know about the time you claimed you were going camping with the girls, but really, you went camping with Jackson for the weekend."

I didn't know what to say, and I did my best to hide my shocked face, but I also knew that the blush on my cheeks confirmed she was right.

"You want to know how I knew you were seeing him again?"

I nodded.

"Because, my dear, for the first time in years, I saw you smile again. You were finally happy, and you seemed at peace with yourself. The only time you've been like that was when you were with him."

"I've been happy," I said defensively.

"Really? Could have fooled me. Every time I've spoken to you over the last few years, it's been nothing but complaints. Complaining about the job, about Jim, about every single solitary thing going on in your life. Until recently, that is. I know he is the only difference in your life. So, my dear, do yourself a favor, give yourself a break, and allow yourself to be happy, truly happy."

I blinked away my tears and looked over at my mom, who looked down at the wreath on top of the gravestone. Then I looked at the name written on the headstone, and a wave of guilt fell over me.

"Mom." I choked, a heavy feeling coming over me.

"Why my dear?"

"How can I be happy when my brother is dead? You do not know how much guilt I carry from that night." I buried my face in my hands and fought back the sobs I felt coming on.

"Honey, it's time to let it go. Your brother wouldn't want you to live your life this way. He'd want you to be happy. You need to honor his memory by living your life, not by racking yourself with guilt over his death."

"But, Mom, it's all my fault."

My mom became blurry as my eyes welled with tears, which I quickly wiped away.

"Bailey, we've talked about this many times, and I will not tell you anything you haven't already heard. You didn't do anything wrong. You were out with the girls."

"I know, but that night we ran into them outside of the bars. They were supposed to be doing security checks. They were almost finished, and Cara and I asked Jackson and Ryan to stay and hang with us for a few minutes."

"And you think this is your fault? How?"

"Connor wouldn't stay. He said he'd go finish doing the security checks and come back."

"So, you think because Ryan and Jackson stayed with you girls, that was the reason he died?"

I nodded, tears streaming down my face.

"If they had been with him, he wouldn't have needed to radio for backup when he came across the door that was open. There would have been three of them there when the guy came running out of the building." I could barely understand my own words as sobs wracked my body.

I felt Mom's arms around me as she pulled me into her. "You need to let that all go, baby girl. Just let it all go," she whispered as she rubbed my back. "None of this was anyone's fault."

"You're wrong."

Mom let me go and placed her hands on my upper arms. "Bailey, listen to me and listen well. I could go on blaming all kinds of people for what happened that night. I could blame Ryan, Jackson, or even Dave Specter for putting the three of them on that duty. It's not going to get me anywhere, and it's not going to bring Connor back here. Just like you are blaming yourself, but that isn't going to bring him back, and it's not going to solve anything. It's only going to bring you a long life of misery. It's no way for anyone to live."

I hugged my mom tight, and as her words sunk in, soon the tears stopped, but the heaviness in my chest remained.

"Bailey, I never told you this, but your brother was so happy that you were with Jackson. I remember the day he'd found out you were engaged. He played it up like he was upset, and that his best friend stole his sister, but after you went to bed that night, he confided in me. He was so proud of you for accepting his proposal. He told me that out of all the guys you dated, Jackson was the only one he didn't want to beat up."

"Why are you telling me this?" I whispered.

Mom stepped back. "Because I think you need to hear it. I also think it's time I leave the two of you alone," she said, pushing the strands of hair from my eyes. "So, you can sort some things out."

"Who, me and Connor?" I questioned.

"No." She smiled. "You and Jackson." She nodded behind me.

I turned, surprised to see Jackson standing a little way up the hill behind me, watching us, then turned back to face my mother.

"Bailey, be nice. It's Christmas. Give the guy a break." She winked, leaning in and placing a kiss on my cheek.

My mom picked up the fall wreath and patted me on the shoulder as she walked by me and over to him. They exchanged some words, and then he leaned in and kissed her cheek. We both watched her as she went and sat over on a bench in the middle of the cemetery. Jackson turned and slowly made his way over to me.

"How did you get here?" I asked, worried that he might have gotten behind the wheel of his truck when I knew he had been told he shouldn't be driving.

"Ryan brought me."

"Oh. How did you know I'd be here?"

Jackson looked to the ground before meeting my eyes. "I didn't expect to see you here at all. Your Mom never spends this day alone, Bailey. I've made sure of that for the past five years. No matter what, I am always here. I spend the morning, afternoon, or evening with her. If it's the morning, we come here, and then I take her out for breakfast. Sometimes, Ryan joins us, but he had some work-related things he had to do this morning, so he asked me to tell your mom he was sorry he couldn't make it. That's what I told her before she went and sat down. Normally, I meet her here at eight, but I was running a little late this morning."

I didn't know what to say to his admission. I did not

know that he had been doing this for the past five years. "Why has Mom never mentioned it to me?"

"Because I didn't want you to know, so I asked her not to say anything," he said, looking at the ground. "If you think you're the only one who carries guilt around with you, you're wrong, Bailey."

I didn't know what to say. I looked into the blue eyes I'd loved so much and saw a mountain of emotion. "Is that what the nightmares are about? That night?"

Jackson looked at me and I feared he was once again not going to tell me, but he surprised me by nodding. "Every single one. They are always the same. I watch the whole thing happen as I am running towards them, but feel like I get nowhere. I didn't get there in time. Now, the nightmares remind me I let us fall apart."

"You didn't let us fall apart," I whispered.

"Didn't I? The night of the shooting, I promised your brother right before he died that I'd always look after you. When things got tough between us, I let him down. So, it's not only the guilt of me not being there to help him when he needed us, but now it's the guilt of breaking my promise to him. I can't protect you and keep you safe when we aren't together."

"Is that what you were dreaming about the other night?" I questioned.

"Yes. They've been worse this year than ever.

Although, aside from the one night, they've all stopped the nights you were with me, except for that one."

"Really."

"Yes," Jackson said, stepping in closer to me. "With you around, they are almost non-existent. I know you hate my job. I know you hate the fact I'm in danger, but it's what I signed up to do. I love my job, just like your brother loved his."

I felt the tears well in my eyes again. I went to turn away to hide my face from him, but Jackson wouldn't allow it. He stepped in and wrapped his arms tightly around me, pulling me against him.

"I know," I whimpered.

"Bailey, do me a favor and just let it all go," he whispered to me as he held me in his arms. "Let it go so we can have the chance that we deserve. He'd want us to be happy."

He held me in the safety of his arms as I cried, letting go of all the guilt I carried from the night of brother's death. He didn't let me go when I'd quieted down either, instead he just continued to hold me.

"I don't want you to leave," he whispered, kissing my forehead.

"I don't want to leave either," I said, looking up into his eyes.

"Then don't. Stay here and marry me," he said, leaning down and meeting my lips for a quick kiss. "Marry me like you were supposed to." He whispered, his lips grazing mine again.

I looked into his eyes. "Are you kidding?"

He shook his head. "Bailey, I want to spend my life with you. That's all I've ever wanted. That's why I waited for you."

"Jackson..." I placed my hands on his chest, not sure how I was supposed to respond.

"Look, I know this isn't the perfect place to ask you. A cemetery isn't the place for this, and I promise in a few days I'll take you someplace more romantic and get down on one knee. For now, though, you need to know that I mean it. I want to spend the rest of my life with you."

His words hit me all at once. Marrying him was all I ever wanted deep down as well.

"I love you, Bailey."

"I love you too, and yes, I will marry you."

Bailey lay in my arms, her eyes closed, drifting in and out of sleep. The warmth from the fire was soothing as one of the worst winter storms Sunset Cove had ever seen raged outside.

We'd had Christmas dinner with her mom, then spent the evening watching movies and sipping on hot cocoa before we'd returned here to our place. I'd built a fire while Bailey brought out a bunch of blankets and pillows from the bedroom, throwing them down on the floor. There we curled up together and watched another movie.

"You are just about asleep." I whispered, kissing the shell of her ear.

"No, I'm okay."

"I call bullshit." I gently nipped the column of her

neck and slid my hand under her shirt, taking in the feeling of her soft, warm skin.

I relished the feeling of her against my body. The soft curves, how she fit against me either way so perfectly. This, having her in my arms, was my Christmas wish come true. I kissed down her neck, to her shoulder while my hand explored her perfectly sized breasts.

"Okay, I'm awake." She giggled, pushing my hand away.

I pulled her in against me and closed my eyes for a moment while my hand that was tucked under the pillow we shared fiddled with the little velvet box. I'd promised her a ring and right after the day in the cemetery, I'd begun shopping when I'd had free time.

I did not know why I was nervous as we lay here together. She'd already said yes, but still I felt she might change her mind.

"You know I love you. That I'm in love with you." I asked, my tone turning from playful to serious.

Bailey rolled in my arms and looked into my eyes, a small frown resting on her face. "Jackson, is...is there something wrong? Of course, I know you love me."

"No, babe, nothing is wrong. I just want to make sure you know that."

"Well, I'll say it again. Of course, I know that. You know I too love you."

I'd told myself after everything that we'd been through

that I'd never not tell her. I wanted to make sure she knew she was wanted, and loved, and that together no matter what we'd faced in the lifetime, that we'd do it together.

I fiddled with the box, and reached around her, kissing her while I slipped it from my left hand to my right and slipped it into the pocket of my jeans.

"I'm just going to run to the washroom."

"Okay, I'll be waiting." She grinned, kissing me one more time before I left.

I stood in the bathroom, leaning on the sink while I looked at myself in the mirror. It was time to claim what I'd wanted by making it official. I reached into my pocket and pulled out the small white velvet box, and opened it up. I looked down at the ring, praying she loved it.

I opened the door to the bathroom, and stepped back into the living room, surprised to find Bailey had gotten up from where we'd laid together.

"Hey, where are you?" I called.

"Grabbing us some drinks, be right out."

I smiled to myself and made my way back over to where we'd been laying together and kneeled down before she'd come back in. I'd just gotten into position when she returned, a soft smile on her face as she brought over two mugs of hot cocoa.

Smiling, I waited for her to place them down. When she turned around, she looked at me, laughter in her eyes.

"What are you doing sitting like that?" She asked, taking me in.

I said nothing, I just stared up at her, while I rested on my one knee.

"Jackson, come on…what are you doi…"

The words hadn't even left her lips, but I knew she'd just clued into what was going on. I reached for my pocket and pulled out that small box, while tears came to her eyes.

She covered her mouth and met my eyes, while she, too, dropped to her knees.

"Jackson…"

"Bailey Scott. Love of My Life. Will you do me the extraordinary honor of becoming my wife?" I flipped the box open and waited for her answer.

She didn't even look at the ring, instead she brought both her hands to my cheeks and pressed her lips against mine.

"A million times, yes." She murmured between kisses.

Our lips parted, and I carefully removed the ring, taking her hand in mine. I slipped the ring on her finger. She sat there, staring down at it, tears falling from her eyes. "I love it." She whispered, "Almost as much as I love you."

I smiled and pulled her against me for another kiss, my tongue parting her lips, washing through her mouth.

# Bailey

A Year Later

I grabbed the last bag of groceries from the car, resting it on my hip as I shut the door. I was just about to head into the house when Jackson pulled into the driveway and cut the engine.

"Hey, sweetie, let me carry that for you." He climbed out of the car and came around, taking the bag from me, then pressing his lips to mine. "How are you feeling today?"

I rested my hand on my barely protruding belly and smiled. "Fine. A little tired, but good."

We'd been married for six months and had found out we were expecting a month later.

Jackson leaned in to kiss me again, this time placing his hand on top of mine just in time to feel the baby kick.

"Did you feel that?" he questioned, and then laughed. "My son's already trying to bust out of there."

"Your son? What if it's a girl?"

Jackson looked at me as if I were being ridiculous. "Not a chance. Did you feel that kick? That's all boy in there."

"Come on, we should get inside. The ice cream is in that bag, and I've been craving it all day. I'd like it not to melt by the time I sit down to have some. You can help me put the groceries away."

"Just what I want to do." He winked, kissing my cheek and led me inside.

After we put away the groceries, I made us each a hot chocolate while Jackson fired up the barbeque. He loved to grill, even in the winter. I sat at the table and began reading the newspaper I'd picked up.

"Just going to get the potatoes on the grill," he said, kissing the top of my head.

The doorbell rang, and Jackson ran out front to get it. I could hear him laughing and knew immediately it had to be someone from work. I listened as he chuckled, but then his voice turned serious. I hated it when I heard that tone in his voice and did my best to shut it out.

I'd just flipped open the newspaper to the next section

and was about to read the next article when Jackson stepped back into the kitchen.

"One of the guys?" I questioned.

"It was Ryan."

"Oh, Cara said he was working tonight. That's odd, he'd be stopping by. Is everything okay?" I looked up to see a serious look on his face.

"What is it?"

"They arrested Garrick Barton this afternoon. He apparently jacked a car at gunpoint. Ryan said they just went and picked him up. He's in custody."

Jackson had eventually told me all that he knew about Garrick. He told me how the bullets at my brother's shooting had matched the one the doctors had removed from him. He had told me that Dorian had cracked under pressure the night they arrested him, and he had turned Garrick in, giving the police everything they needed to know. The only problem was Garrick had run and hadn't been seen again.

"What?" I asked in disbelief. I didn't know what to do or say at this news. Finding the man responsible for my brother had been something I'd been praying for since the day he died.

"They got him, babe. It's over," Jackson said, coming up behind me and wrapping his arms around me.

I tried hard not to cry, but with all the hormones that

were flooding my body, it was impossible not to. "We've got to go tell Mom," I said, standing up.

"Better yet, we'll cook all the food and take dinner over."

I lay in bed reading the first chapter of a new book when Jackson walked in, towel wrapped around his waist. I couldn't help but peek over the top of my book as my fiancé dropped the towel from his body and made his way over to the bed.

"Give it up, would you?" He chuckled. "I know you're pretending to read, but in reality, you're checking me out."

I rolled my eyes. "Okay, whatever. When did you become so full of yourself?" I giggled.

"Since you came back," he said, throwing the covers down on his side of the bed and crawling in.

I placed my book on my bedside table, shut the light off, and snuggled down under the covers and into his arms.

"Did you see your mom's face tonight when we told her?"

"I know. She looked like she wanted to cheer and cry."

I said, thinking back to when we had shared the news with her.

I closed my eyes and rested my head on Jackson's chest, taking in his fresh scent.

"What are you thinking about?" he asked as his hands trailed down and rested on my lower back.

"You," I murmured.

"Is that so?"

I nodded. Jackson rolled me onto my back and looked down into my face. He placed his lips on mine and kissed me hard. I could feel him growing hard against me and pushed him away, laughing. "What are you doing?"

"What do you think I'm doing?" he asked as his hands wandered over my body.

I stopped laughing when I caught the look in his eyes. He slowly brought his lips to mine, then he reached up and shut the light off, bathing the room in darkness.

I slipped from the bed in the early morning and wandered down the hall to the kitchen. I quietly made myself a cup of tea and sat down in my favorite chair in the living room. I flipped the lights on the tree and pulled a blanket over my legs.

I loved early mornings like this, especially at this time of the year. I always welcomed the quietness. It gave me time to reflect on things. It was Christmas Eve; we had a busy day ahead of us, visiting my mom and then Cara and Ryan.

The last year, especially after our wedding, I'd spent a lot of time to focus on healing. Things were falling into place in my life and once I found out that we were going to have a baby, I knew I needed to be there for him or her in my entirety.

The things I put into practice, Jackson also put into practice. We both learned to talk to one another, especially when things were tough. We'd gone through a lot together and communication had been our weakness. We'd gone to see a therapist together and worked through those weaknesses, each of us learning things about ourselves along the way.

I picked up my tea and took a sip. I leaned my head back against the chair and took a deep breath. Letting him go had been the hardest thing I'd ever had to do, but it was ultimately what had led us back to one another. Our therapist told us that sometimes you must let go of what you love, as hard as it may be, to see if it will be returned to you. If not, then it wasn't meant to be.

Luckily for me, and for Jackson, we each returned to one another, and our love was now stronger than ever.

# GET TWO FREE BOOKS

Sign up for my newsletter and I'll send you two FREE books.

https://geni.us/NLSignupBackMatter

Follow S.L. Sterling

Did you know that bookbub has a feature where you can follow me and it will send you an alert when I release a book or put a title on sale? Sign up here and make sure you stay in the loop.

Bookbub:
https://geni.us/SLSterlingBookbub

Website
https://www.authorslsterling.com

Facebook
https://geni.us/SLSterlingFB

Twitter
https://geni.us/SLSterlingTwitter

Instagram
https://geni.us/SLSterlingInstagram

Tiktok
https://geni.us/slsterlingtiktok

Reader Group

USA Today Bestselling Author S.L. Sterling was born and raised in southern Ontario.

An avid reader all her life, S.L. Sterling dreamt of becoming an author. She decided to give writing a try after one of her favorite authors launched a course on how to write your novel. This course gave her the push she needed to put pen to paper and her debut novel "It Was Always You" was born.

When S.L. Sterling isn't writing or plotting her next novel she can be found curled up with a cup of coffee, blanket and the newest romance novel from one of her favorite authors.

In her spare time, she enjoys camping, hiking, sunny destinations, spending quality time with family and friends and of course reading.

To be notified of new releases or sales, join S.L. Sterling's private Mailing List.
https://geni.us/NLSignupBackMatter

Get even more of the inside scoop when you join S.L. Sterling's private Facebook group, Sterling's Silver Sapphires: https://geni.us/SapphiresReaderGroup

# Other Books by S.L. Sterling

It Was Always You

On A Silent Night

Bad Company

Back to You this Christmas

Fireside Love

Holiday Wishes

Saviour Boy

The Boy Under the Gazebo

The Greatest Gift

Into the Sunset

Letting You Go

**The Spencer Brooks Diaries**

Our Little Secret

Our Little Surprise

Our Little Wedding

**The Malone Brother Series**

A Kiss Beneath the Stars

In Your Arms

His to Hold

Finding Forever with You

**Vegas MMA**

Dagger

**The Doctors of Eastport General**

Doctor Desire

Doctor Right

Doctor Frost

All I Want for Christmas (Contemporary Romance Holiday
Collection)

**Willow Valley**

Memories of the Past

To Trust My Heart

Letters from the Heart

What Once was Broken

Scars on my Heart

Vancouver Dominators

Inside the Penalty Box

Ten Minute Misconduct